You Don't Know Who You Are
Until You've Gone Too Far

LEAH HOLBROOK SACKETT

You Don't Know Who You Are Until You've Gone Too Far

– SHORT STORIES –

All rights reserved. Published by New Meridian, part of the non-profit organization New Meridian Arts, 2021.

LIBRARY OF CONGRESS CATALOGING-IN-PUBLICATION DATA

You Don't Know Who You Are Until You've Gone Too Far
Authored by Leah Holbrook Sackett
ISBN: 9781737249139
LCCN: 2021950145

For my family,
champions of the written word.

Contents

Where Grief Fits In

Incarceration Nation

Acknowledgements

If I Could Cry, I'd Be Happier in Secret Attic Issue #15

Liquor Shack in Backchannels

The Sound of Mischief in Sirens Call Publishing

Stained Sheets upcoming in Literatus

Lip Blam in Goat's Milk

Hello Laura in Arkansan Review

How to Make Waffles Like Mom in Brown Bag
Journal and in White Knight Escort Service

Spooning Award Winner in Art Ascent

Unchanged Bedclothes in Tigershark Publishing

What the Looking Glass Reflects in Mum Life Stories

Days of Bacon in Pure Slush

The Rome Club in Adelaide Magazine

Suicide Culture in Tiny Molecule

Dictation of a Drowning in Fahmidan Journal

Where Grief Fits In

On The Hunt, On the Lamb

WALTER AND BRIDGET WERE HAVING A good time on an ugly couch with Great Aunt Judy. The brown floral pattern swept and climbed over the dated sofa. The seats should have sagged under the weight of the years, but no one visited Great Aunt Judy, and she never sat on her prize couch. Great Aunt Judy favored the brown corduroy recliner by the window. Walter and Great Aunt Judy had coffee, and Bridget had some quick fix Swiss Miss cocoa with marshmallows. It was an excellent start for a hunting trip, thought Bridget. Great Aunt Judy had every confidence in the pending success of the deer hunt. Bridget's mom had been uneasy about letting Walter take their daughter to northwest Colorado on a hunting trip. Amy protested that Bridget was a girl and too young. Bridget bristled at the objection.

"I'm not too young," Bridget protested. "I am 12, and Dad was 9 on his first hunting trip."

"Well, he's a boy," Amy said.

As soon as she said it, she regretted it. Here Amy had been teaching Bridget the importance of being a feminist. She'd started with the HBO Original Gloria Steinem: In Her Own Words, and she'd subscribed them to B*tch Media. But when it came down to guns and hunting, she was a hypocrite. So, Amy bit her tongue and waved goodbye to Walter and Bridget as they backed out of the driveway in his red F-150. By the time Walter and Bridget made it to Great Aunt Judy's, Bridget had forgotten all about the argument with her mother. She was just too excited about the father-daughter time. Their first stop had been for dinner at a Denny's just outside of Kansas. Dad let her order off the adult menu. Bridget forced herself to eat every bite because she didn't want Dad to feel like he wasted his money. When they got to Great Aunt Judy's small clapboard house in a wasteland of dirt, Bridget began to feel like she was on a grand adventure. Inside the small living room, looking over a stack of photo albums piled high on the floor. Bridget studied the black and white faces of all the Englund's that had come before. She felt like a solid link in a never-ending chain of people, connected as one. Each face like a fin-gerprint with whorls and arches, the captured smiles and frowns from squinting into the sun, from a life of hard work burned into immortality on film.

"This album is mostly your dad and Uncle," Great Aunt Judy said.

Bridget wiped the cocoa from her upper lip with her shirt sleeve and made an eager dive into the snapshots of her dad at her age. By this album, color photos peered back at Bridget's ardent gaze. She looked intently at the boy who would become her father. She looked just like him, apart from the braids. The photos' entertainment wore thin with the sinking sun, and both Bridget and Walter were itching to get back on the road. As they said their goodbyes, Great Aunt Judy removed a porcelain angel she had painted from a shelf behind the recliner and placed it in the palm of Bridget's hand.

"To bless you on your journey," Great Aunt Judy said.

It was ivory with gold trim and faceless, which made it a little creepy, but it was at the same time, pretty. Bridget sensed her dad stiffen with Aunt Judy's religious outreach, with the advent of the angel, so Bridget stuffed it into her right pocket.

Departing at this hour, they would have to get a motel room because it would be too dark to set up camp. Bridget was okay with another diversion; it meant Dad would let her raid the vending machine. Bridget ate enough junk food to put her in a food coma. However, she did have an entire bag of Cheetos leftover, which she stuffed into the inside pocket of her deer hunting coat draped across a rattan chair. The Motel room was gross. It was last updated and cleaned in the 70s. Walter told Bridget to sleep on top of the covers.

They rose with the sun and drove into Basalt and Roaring Fork Valley. Bridget was anxious to use her new gun. Dad had bought her rifle at Cabela's. It was a Savage Arms Axis XP Bolt-Action Rifle in True-Timber Strata Camo. It was a mouthful, and it was all hers. Riding in the front seat of Dad's F-150, Bridget slid her hunter's license from her Hello Kitty wallet.

She had a license to hunt before a license to drive. She was thrilled.

Walter parked the car in the lot. They were going to hike the rest of the way into camp. Bridget carried a lighter load than her dad, but after 3 miles, she was missing her Nintendo Switch and the living room couch. Walter sensed Bridget's waning enthusiasm and began telling her glory stories of the hunt. Underneath each word, he wondered if Amy was right about Bridget's age and gender. Once camp was made, Walter tutored Bridget to make a fire and pitch a tent; then, he got to the exciting part. How to shoot her rifle. Bridget was a natural. Her aim was good, but she complained about the kickback of the gun. Her shoulder was sore, and Bridget figured she'd have to get a good shot off quick tomorrow because she could sense her lack of stamina. The rest of the afternoon, Bridget gathered sticks that could be burned in the fire; then, she sat on a log and ate Cheetos while nursing her tender shoulder. The noises of the animals kept Bridget awake that night. She tried to catalog each sound, but the sounds were new. The only animal she'd had any close proximity to was her tuxedo cat, KC. Bridget snuggled up to her sleeping dad's back. Close to sunrise, Bridget nodded off, just to be awakened by her dad. It was time.

They had hiked another couple of miles into the woods. She walked behind her dad with her loaded rifle slung over her good shoulder. The weight was pleasing, even if the Camo was unappealing. Walter came to a stop; Bridget strode up beside him.

"Do you hear something?" she said.

"Shh. Whisper."

"Did you hear something?" she whispered.

"I thought so. Let's stop here for a moment and check this clearing."

They lay on their stomachs at the edge of the brush and waited. Bridget's heart was pounding, but the waiting eventually took the edge off. She tried to shift her position. But her dad steadied her movements with a hand on the shoulder.

"There's a deer at the other side of the clearing moving this way," he said.

Bridget looked, but she didn't see anything until it moved further out of the brush. It was a 10-point buck. It was beautiful.

"Okay, get ready. Just like I taught you," Dad said.

Suddenly, the gun felt bulky and heavy. Bridget squeezed her eyes shut and prayed for a good shot. She was pumped with adrenaline and did not heed Walter's next round of directions. She let off a shot, and the deer dropped after the slightest hesitation.

Bridget couldn't believe it. She did it. She shot a deer. Walter was also dumbfounded. Carefully, although Bridget was primed to move with haste, Walter and Bridget closed the distance between them and the deer. Absorbed in the glassy-eyed deer, Bridget failed to hear the dry, crunching steps of another. When she clued into the sound, she expected to see another deer, but it was a large man with a scraggly dark blond beard. His blue eyes were penetrating and darted between her dad, the deer, and herself. His mouth was anchored tight in a grimace. The clearing rocked a deathlike quiet that staggered in with the mysterious man.

"Hello," Walter said and extended his hand.

"You g-g-got me b-buck," the man said, snubbing the handshake.

"Um, it is her buck," Walter said.

Walter rose to a standing position with his weight balanced across both feet, shoulder's width apart, but his stance was reduced in the bulking frame of the stranger. Bridget stood behind her dad with her rifle. The intruder eyed Bridget. Bridget made a mental sketch of the man from his stutter to his stubbly chin and his droopy left eyelid. He looked rough, like he'd been living in the woods a long time.

"Yeah, her b-buck," he said and turned away.

They watched him leave to the right side of the clearing.

"What was that about?" Bridget asked.

"I think that's what we call a sore loser," Walter whispered. "Keep your voice down. It will carry across the clearing."

Walter taught Bridget how to field dress a deer through whispered directions and grunts with the gutting knife. She moved back a few steps as her dad positioned the deer belly-up and pointed the hind end toward the downward slope in the clearing.

"You want to let gravity help drain the blood," he said without looking at his daughter.

Bridget had understood they were going to kill a deer, but she had no prior experience that could prepare her for hacking up a large animal. Her adrenaline was ramping up again. She was nauseated and wanted to run back to the brush, the camp, the car, and home. But she was stuck in the dry grass kneeling in a patch now wet with blood. The world seemed sluggish as she watched her dad remove a foldable saw from his backpack. If he had glanced in her direction during the gutting and removal of the organs, he would have found a piqued child.

"Now, I'm going to use the Wyoming saw to split the sternum. Then I'm going to release the diaphragm and cut the windpipe," he said.

She was silent, kneeling with her butt resting on her heels and the blood-soaked knees of her jeans feeling cold and itchy. Her father's words sank into the bloody earth. They were lost on her. Bridget felt like her head was a balloon floating away over the field. While her dad continued to pull out the deer's innards and place them in a pile to the side of the deer, she fought back the tears. She didn't want him to see that this father-daughter excursion was a mistake.

Walter continued to give dressing instructions and point out the meat they would keep. He handed the bloody knife to Bridget and instructed her on making a cut; he finally noticed her distress. He told her about the excellent venison meatloaf recipe he'd gotten from Great Aunt Judy, which would go great with what was left of his homemade Meade. He'd even let her have a little sip; after all, this was her kill. Walter was beaming with pride.

Walter gave Bridget a quick hug and smeared blood across the shoulder of her coat. They packed in the meat to hike out. Despite it being wasteful, Walter decided not to make multiple trips to carry all the meat out. One look at Bridget's face, and he knew she couldn't take much more of this hunting trip. Perhaps Amy had been right.

As they made their way back to camp, Walter sensed they were being followed. They paused on the trail, and he looked behind them.

"Wait here," Walter said.

"Where are you going?" Bridget asked.

Walter did not answer; he just handed her his gun. He walked several feet and climbed an elephant-sized boulder, but he did not reach the top. The rock was smooth and had no footholds or handholds. He came crashing down and busted his ankle. There was a bulge of a broken bone underneath the skin.

"Dad!" Bridget exclaimed.

After calling out to him, she had fainted at the sight of his blood. When she came to, her dad was lying unconscious, and at the time, she thought he was dead. She roused him by shaking his shoulders and pounding on his chest amidst her angry tears. When he regained consciousness, he told her he was going into shock, and she had to go get help. But help was a half day's hike away. Walter was in too much pain to shush her crying.

"Shit. God Damn it," Walter said, none too quiet.

"Dad, can't you just walk a little?" Bridget asked.

She knelt beside him. After her dad took a breather, he asked her to help him up. But he slumped back to the ground with a new round of curse words.

"Bridget, I can't put weight on this ankle. It's broken. You're going to have to go get help," he said. His blood-stained hands gripped her by the shoulders. There was more blood in this day than a Steven King made for TV movie, thought Bridget.

"What? No," she said. "I can't do that."

"Bridget, I need you to do this for me. I can't walk. You have to be a big girl and do this," Walter said.

He instructed her to follow the trail and keep checking for a signal on his phone. He uncertainly reminded her to steer clear of the hunter. He didn't want to scare her even more, but he felt she needed to know.

"Now go on, you can do this," he said.

His voice was a little firmer than he had intended, but he needed to push her. He knew this entire day was outside her comfort zone, but there was nothing he could do about it now. Bridget kissed her dad goodbye, slung her rifle over her shoulder, and mustered up the courage to walk away.

Bridget had not hiked too far before she sat in the dirt, leaning back against a blue spruce just a few paces off the trail. She sat in a spill of pine needles, and she picked them up and rolled them between her fingers. Bridget felt like she could not go on. She had come to a stop. Her self-pity was a thin shelter like the tree. Her sight of the path was blurred by tears and sunlight. Bridget expected it was high noon. Her adventure had been snagged and unraveled by the interference of a crazy hunter. She didn't even want that damn deer. The heavy stench of it was in her backpack. Bridget took a deep breath and vomited across her sleeve and into the dirt. She knew she had to make it to the ranger's station to get help. But she hadn't paid that much attention to their hike in. Bridget looked up into the towering blue spruce and started climbing the 90-foot tree.

Taking on one sturdy branch at a time, climbing higher and higher into the blue spruce, she got only 15 feet off the ground when she saw a man moving down the trail from where she had come. It was him. It was the crazy hunter, and he was tracking her. Bridget wrapped herself around the tree, her climbing arrested by fear. The hunter stopped just 5 feet off from the blue spruce. Bridget was sure he could smell her fear or the deer meat strapped to her back. She fretted he would hear her heart pounding in her chest. She was afraid of dying, really dying like the deer. Her hot tears rolled down her cheeks in silence. Before this hunt, her tears had been accompanied by loud cries spilled in her mother's arms. This trip had taught her how to cry alone. Finally, the hunter moved off. He was backtracking. Bridget wondered if he had found her dad or if he would, and she was afraid of what he would do to her injured father.

Bridget's arms and legs were beginning to tingle. She needed to climb down. She couldn't see the hunter from her perch, and he'd been gone a long time. With her rifle strapped to her back, she began the long descent. The bark left scratches in her sweaty palms. Her grip was precarious; still, she did not know what she feared more—falling or the crazed hunter. Bridget thought about doubling back to her dad without help, but she knew she had to go on alone. Dad needed medical attention.

All of this had seemed daunting enough, and now the hunter was tracking her. Bridget was crumbling under the weight of the day. Hope seemed out of reach as she waited in the branches of the spruce. She waited for strength or courage to come like in a book with a flip of the page, the qualities of a hero would be bestowed upon her. She watched the trembling aspens dancing in the wind. She knew it was going to get cold at night. She had to move. Bridget did her best to put her feelings aside. Then she realized it was her fear that propelled her forward despite the obstacles. She had to continue to outpace the hunter and the sun. Yes, she was armed, but if killing a deer left her wrecked, then she could never pull the trigger on a person. The gun was no good to her.

Bridget finally climbed all the way down from her perch with a good idea of the direction she needed to be going. She picked up her pace and stopped feeling sorry for herself. She must get to the ranger. It was with relief that Bridget stumbled into her and dad's camp with the banked fire and the orange pup tent. But the tent was deflated, and broken stakes were strewn about. The ax was missing from the stack of wood. Water had been poured on the fire. Somehow, the hunter had beaten her here. Bridget spun in circles looking for the crazed man. She clutched her gun in her left hand. This tool of death for the deer was her only defense from a madman.

Bridget was unsure of her next move. She did not have the decision and confidence of her father. Bridget stood silent, closed her eyes, and listened. Off to the right, she heard water, rushing water. Bridget moved off toward Frying Pan River. She thought the sound of the water could camouflage her movements. She remembered how the river ran close to the parking lot, car, and ranger's station. Bridget breached a 30-foot drop-off and carefully started a descent to the water's edge. The rock was brittle even under her small frame. She moved slowly, and she slid as much as she climbed down the cliff. Once on the rocky shore, Bridget drank handfuls of clear water. Her hands grew bone-cold in the running water, so she shoved them in her pockets. Bridget felt the little porcelain angel in her right pocket. She withdrew the angel from the sanctuary of her coat, and it glinted in the sun. It was a beacon. Bridget whispered a prayer looking for guidance and protection, and she named her fragile angel Grace with a kiss on the smooth blank face.

On the shoreline of the wild roaring river, Bridget realized she was standing in the open. She would be an easy target, so she found a spot masked in the limbs of another Colorado Blue Spruce. Bridget squatted and pulled out her rifle to use the eyeglass to size up her environment. She would venture back out if all were peaceful and follow the Frying Pan River down to the ranger's station. A crack sounded above in the rock face. Bridget heard him before she saw him. She looked up to see the hunter. Instinctively, she held her breath. He stood at the cliff edge, searching for her. He carried his rifle in hand like an extension of himself, and he began to climb down. She watched his worn brown leather hiking boots patched with duct tape and laced in hot pink laces through her site. He stepped too quickly and lost his footing on the loose shale. He fell from the top of the rock face, and he could do nothing to brace himself with the gun in his hand. His bulky body fell 30 feet to the bottom, and he landed with a sickening crack. Bridget waited for him to get up. After several minutes, Bridget rose to her feet. She stuffed the angel, Grace, back into her pocket. Eventually, she crept out from her hiding spot. Her gun was cocked and aimed.

"Are you okay?" she asked.

She was met with silence. Bridget slowly closed the gap with her rifle in hand. Then she saw it. A pool of dark blood spreading out onto the shoals, emanating from the back of the man's head. His dead eyes were open. Bridget stood guard and cried. She had just prayed for him to be gone, dead. But Bridget didn't really mean it. She just wanted to be safe. Bridget was like a sentinel to death. A death she felt she managed. In her steadfast position, she let the moment hurt. Bridget was afraid to move from the dead man, to turn her back. Maybe he wasn't dead. Her day had been maimed and marred by death. She could see nothing valiant about hunting. She'd much rather go with her mother to buy meat at the grocery store. The day waxed on indifferent to her plight. The sun was retreating in the sky. It was not going to heed her prayers. With a sinking feeling, Bridget watched the sun go down. Before the light faded completely, she unbagged the deer meat in her backpack, put it on the hunter's chest, and wrapped his hands around it. He had wanted that deer so badly; it had cost him his life.

Bridget had to move. She certainly did not want to be caught in the dark with this body. The cliff face, now truly ominous, was a no-go for Bridget. She hiked down alongside the water. She was determined to get help for her father. But in the fragile light of the moon, Bridget tripped and fell. There was a snap and a poking into her ribs. It wasn't penetration, but she had fallen on something sharp. She heard it when she sat up—the sharp slide of porcelain shards. Bridget pulled out the little angel. Grace had a broken wing. She was wounded, and Bridget felt guilty about the broken angel. The angel had protected her, even if at too high a price.

Bridget looked at Grace, and she thought of throwing her into the river, but the longer she looked at it, the more the faceless angel began to look like herself. Unformed, miniature brought to life out of love and death. Wasn't that who Bridget was? The faceless angel called out to Bridget. Go, Go. But go where? She was trapped like a little figurine, and any movement meant breakage. Bridget decided to make a small camp on the bank under the moonlight and next to the dark water. A place to shelter just long enough until she could see again to continue her trek.

There had been a gloss, a shine to life before this day. Life was filled with that new doll smell and promised fairytale adventure, glorious and unreal. The days before were not raw, like today. Today, life had ripped open, proving reality to be a gash, a gaping wound that even a parent could not brush away. Her father's dependence on her to save his life was unfair. The boundaries of her existence had been blown to pieces when she shot that deer. The hunting had felt like a game, all the way up to the dressing. The gore, the blood smeared in the tall grass, on her father's hands, and on her own were someplace other than she had ever been before. Bridget knew there was no going back. Then the hunter had appeared a surreal menace in the heat of the sun. His demeanor, a demand in itself, reflected his desire. He was a force to be reckoned with, his envy an insurmountable lust and hate.

"It was a damn deer," Bridget said under her breath. She had mourned the deer and the crazed hunter long enough. She had to seek help for her dad. Bridget didn't know how much time she had, but she knew she needed to hurry, and this dead man had taken up too much time already. In the moonlight, Bridget set off following the roaring river again. She kept Dad's cell phone handy to check for a signal, but there was none in that valley. Bridget considered looking for a place to climb back up, but after the hunter's fall, she wasn't keen on climbing anymore.

The moonlight shone off the water in a fickle fashion. It winked when blocked by the shadows of the trembling aspens. Bridget wondered if a ranger would even be present in the night. She thought about what her dad was doing, waiting for her all this time. Her faith in herself was growing with every rocky step. She would succeed. She had to. At the bend in the river, the phone was dying. Bridget wished she were at home. She wished she had survival skills. Her wishes got her nowhere, but her steady plodding and hopeful monologue whispered in the dark built an armor of bravery.

When Bridget approached the ranger station at a run, she had no idea the time. The phone was long dead. Her hope bled into disbelief that she had reached her destination. Bridget was fearful the station would fade away in front of her, but her commotion had roused the park ranger who met her at the door. Quickly, but not quick enough for Bridget, a team was assembled.

Bridget was given a granola bar and water while waiting for the sun to break over a new day.

On the climb back into the woods, the little angel clinked inside her pocket; when they came upon her father, he was rough, but he would be all right. As the men righted Walter and got him on a gurney to carry him out of the woods, they praised Bridget for being a hero. Bridget walked back out of the woods. She wanted to feel relieved or thankful, but these feelings were lost, just out of reach. Bridget felt tight and wound up like a spool of twine, taut like a high wire in a circus act. She felt new and hardened, and yet fragile and glazed like the porcelain angel. Bridget felt like she was carrying her former self in pieces, waiting for a private moment to glue herself back together. Her right hand wrapped around the broken angel in her pocket as she tucked into the ambulance with her father. Looking at his ghostly face, she decided to keep the hunter's fate a secret. Someone would find him. She was done. When Bridget and Walter finally returned home to Amy, Bridget superglued Grace's wing and put her on a shelf.

The Liquor Shack

THE MOONLIT WATERS HELD THE WARMTH from the day. The kids had to communicate in gestures and expressions. Each of them looking down and then quickly away to steal a glimpse of their naked bodies lit by the moon in the quaking waters. The disproportionate bodies submerged in the above-ground pool reflected the cumulative awkwardness of their blooming bodies. The kids had chosen this pool carefully. It was one they knew well. They swam in it, back in the day, years ago, when they were little kids. When they were still friends with the owner, Jimmy. The kids knew the pool was located on the opposite end of the bedrooms of the house. Their risk of getting caught was significantly reduced, thanks to Jimmy's father not wanting to hear the kids while he slept until late in the afternoons. His night shift at the Now and Later candy factory meant he wasn't even home right now, and Mrs. Davis was a heavy sleeper too far away to hear their muted sounds. Sarah liked the way her budding breasts gleamed in the moonlight, so did Aaron. Kristie was too embarrassed to be envious of Sarah.

"Let's play Marco Polo, but quiet like," Aaron said.

The kids all hissed a not-it. Finally, it was decided that Aaron was it. At a later time, these kids would be dubbed tweens. But it was the 80's when childhood lasted longer, and pre-pubescence was a curiosity not yet tainted by a thing called the internet. Their developing bodies were the battlefield of growing up. Their knowledge of their bodies' changes was limited to older siblings' horror stories, parental scratches on a scrap of paper, and an overwhelming yet tantalizing shame.

Aaron centered himself in the pool and closed his eyes. He whispered, "Marco." He heard the swish of the others moving along the circumference of the pool as they mumbled, "Polo." He made a step to his right. That's where he thought Kristie was, and he called again, "Marco." Aaron thrust out his hand underwater and tagged a slick, thick issuance of wet flesh. He flashed open his eyes and found Mark before him. His eagerness faded to defeat. The girls giggled on the other side of the pool, banked against the wall.

"It's your turn," he said to Mark as he backed away. And he realized Mark had let him catch him, so he could be in a position to grab the girls.

As they dressed, Aaron did a poor job of hiding his stare at the girls' glistening white thighs and butts in the moon glow. Mark elbowed him in the ribs and giggled. The girls were suddenly tight-lipped and made their hasty good-bye to head back to Kristie's house. Aaron walked Mark home. Mark was high on the night's nudity and babbled non-stop about the girls' small breasts that had gained three times in size as Mark danced home.

"Oh, we gotta do that again," Mark said to Aaron on the sidewalk in front of Mark's Tudor-style house.

"Shit, yeah," Aaron said and waved Mark goodnight as he crossed the desolate street.

On his way home, his zinging feels from the night's escapade with the girls began to lag as the smell of chlorine lifted from his skin. Home was a mere two blocks from Mark's house, but each step closer grew heavier. Aaron didn't want to go home. When he reached the black door on the lit porch, he couldn't find his key. Aaron checked his wet pockets, but it was gone. He must have lost it when he went skinny dipping. Aaron dropped down into one of the white wicker chairs on the front porch shrinking behind the boxwoods and the lovely scent of the lilac bush. He'd have to wait for his sister, Anna, to show up so he could get in.

Aaron tried to get comfortable in the squeaky chair. He was positioned to watch the driveway for when one of Anna's friends would drive up and drop her drunk ass off. Instead, his gaze drifted to the impenetrable door and the splintered doorjamb. Months ago, Mom went on a cleaning rampage, only days after the funeral. She stamped about the house filling a cardboard box with framed family photos that included dad, his Field and Stream magazines, and his avocado green ashtray on the end table by his recliner. Mom dumped it inside the box, ashes, butts, and all. She eyed the remote control. Then she turned her stony stare on the mossy green recliner. Mom dropped the box and cleared a path from the living room's center to the front door. She heaved the reluctant recliner forward. Aaron sat on the sofa sucking on a blue Tasty Freeze pop, watching, and wondering where her strength came from. His mom got the dang thing all the way to the door before she started cussing.

"This god damn, cheating, son of a bitch," she said through clenched teeth.

"Mom?"

"No. Just no," she said.

His mother stamped from the room. He could hear her in the garage digging around. She'd left the garage door ajar, and he watched the smirking poster of Robert Redford she had taped to the door. There were many pieces of tape on the four corners, all crisscrossed and doing their best to keep the black and white Redford in place. But if someone slammed the door shut, Redford would catch air and pull away from the door, causing another little rip in the poster. Sometimes, when Dad had been drinking, he would remove and hide the poster to aggravate Mom. He thought it was great fun. But, unfortunately, his usual overwhelming, drub nature could not put his propensity asunder for mean spirited pranks while intoxicated.

She returned with a sledgehammer and a saw, and she got to work. The sledgehammer cracked the thing up, but it also caused the wedged recliner to deliver splintery blows to the doorjamb.

"Fuck," she yelled.

Aaron sat with the sucked-out tasty freeze wrapper, which he rolled and unrolled around his pointer finger. With each blow of the sledgehammer, he waited for something to break loose, either the recliner or his mother. Finally, she kicked the chair out into its utmost reclined position and took the saw to it where the back and the seat were connected. The back of the recliner thudded onto the floor, issuing a cloudy aroma of Dad's cigarettes and sweat. When his mom was done hacking the chair to ragged pieces of upholstery, foam, wood, and metal, Aaron asked if he could have a turn.

"No," she said quietly.

Alone, she walked each fragment out to the curb. At some point, she had started crying. Afterward, she started drinking Dad's whiskey. These were the last thoughts Aaron had as he dried and dozed in the wicker chair. He dreamt of his dad. It was always the same. His dad driving the family sedan with a pretty lady with short blond hair sitting in the front seat. It was a pretty day, with no rain. They were cut off by a Home Depot Truck. Dad overcompensated, and the Sedan slid underneath the trailer. His Dad and the lady were decapitated. This is how Dad was caught cheating. In the dream, Aaron always had an up-close view of the bodies in the car. It struck Aaron how much shorter Dad looked without a head.

Aaron jerked awake. It was the only way he woke anymore. Anna still wasn't home. It had to be pretty late, but he didn't know the exact time. It's not like he was going to wear a watch skinny dipping. Tired of waiting for Anna, Aaron got up and stretched. He walked down the driveway, and then he walked 5 doors down, keeping an eye out for his sister. She wasn't there. So, he kept walking, glancing up at the waxing moon. Finally, he walked to the end of the street and made a left. There it was. The same as always.

The Liquor Shack. It was a small white wooden framed shack on a small island of blacktopped space big enough for two cars, which from here looked like a large puddle of darkness. The ramshackle Liquor store was a blight on the otherwise residential area. A streetlamp flooded the liquor shack with a halo of disgraceful illumination. Was it his dad's usual green bottle with the bright yellow label of Cutty Sark from the Liquor shack that led him to drink and drive, or was it drinks at lunch with the bimbo? They would never have a complete picture of the day's events. The missed hours reported from work in the middle of the day, the receipts in the glove box for Coral Courts, a rent by the hour motel, and the blood alcohol content of .22% were the facts left to the family. Aaron tried to puzzle his dad's death into an unfinished and grotesque portrayal of his dad's abandonment of the family.

Standing in the shadows with the warm summer's air kissing his skin, Aaron reflected on the looming Liquor shack. Aaron and Anna had made the walk to the Liquor Shack hundreds of times over the summers.

The Liquor Shack had a small, odd offering. It was four walls of bottles filled with amber or transparent liquid. Next to the register was a shelf of cigarettes, a small bin of lighters, and just by the door was a deep freeze filled with Tasty Freeze popsicles. The siblings were allowed to walk together to the Liquor Shack. They went with the change they dug up out of the sofa and recliner cushions. Mounted on the top of the Liquor Shack was a sign that ran the length of the building, and it read in bold, red All Caps, LIQUOR. Inside the Liquor Shack, it was dark. It would take a moment to adjust their eyes from the brilliant Sun to the cave-like interior of the liquor shack. They would stand for a moment in the doorway, waiting to see, waiting to be ordered out. The man behind the counter always looked angry. Aaron and Anna moved quickly. Trying not to notice the adult world they had stepped into, but they still took the time to fight if there was only one blue popsicle left in the deep freeze. Anna, being the eldest, won every time.

The pavement broke about 200 feet from the shack. The concrete was split and filled with blacktop to create two slight slopes making it wheelchair accessible. In all of Aaron's time walking to the liquor shack, Aaron never saw a wheelchair making its way to the haven of liquor. When he was very little, just out of the stroller, his mom would walk the kids to the shack and back for exercise. She pointed out the flowered stoop of Mrs. Jensen, where Anna and Aaron would race to take a seat and rest as they waited for their mom to catch up.

Mom also pointed out the wheelchair-accessible walk. She would sing out, "down the little hill, up the little hill," every time. The little hills were highlights of the kids' walk to the shack. It was a marker that they were nearly there. Even when Aaron and Anna started walking on their own, under the age of 10, they continued to sing "down the little hill, up the little hill." As Aaron approached the little hills, he sang into the darkness, "down the little hill, up the little hill," and he felt stupid.

The green screen door was unlatched. The white wooden door was kicked in after a few attempts. The sole of Aaron's black high-top converse left a dirty mark. It was pitch black in this place, and it was musty. Aaron walked with his hands out, feeling for the popsicle chest. He knocked a bottle to the floor. The shattering glass sounded excessively loud, and he froze. Nothing happened. His eyes were getting accustomed, and the Cutty Sark label stared up at him from the concrete floor. Aaron grabbed another bottle of Cutty Sark. He opened the screw top and took a swig. His mouth tasted of fiery Nyquil.

How did his parents' drink this stuff? He took several more slugs, and it didn't get better. His throat was burning. Aaron drank until he started to feel numb, and he laughed. It was a choked chuckle, and then he retched. He looked at the bottle in his hand. He faced the joke of his life and hurled the bottle at the wall. More bottles of amber-colored liquid shattered on the floor. The moonlight mixed with the electric humming streetlamp, peeking through the door, and lit up the shards of glass on the floor. Aaron reached out and swung his arms, clearing the shelf before him. The creation of his destruction felt good. He stepped back and admired his damage, and then he turned to the deep freeze. He grabbed a fist full of popsicles and marched home with the gait of an angry young man. Above, the Sun was chasing the moon from the sky. All the blue popsicles were his.

I Can't Save You

I ATE A GIRL SCOUT TODAY. WELL, I ATE 5 BOXES of Samoas and 3 boxes of thin mints. There are 3 boxes of thin mints left in the freezer. I showed some restraint. The Samoas were her favorite; perhaps that was why I couldn't stop eating. I couldn't wait for her to wake out of sedation. The truth is, I didn't want to wait. I was tired of life being on hold. I was hungry. I was starving for the parts of life that make you feel alive, like eating cookies, walking the dog, and dancing. Aspects of a normal life, the little things that constitute living. Instead, we were stuck in a holding pattern, death hovering around, always, like a fly. It buzzed and moved in maddening circles over our heads. I tried striking out with a rolled-up magazine. But death is no ordinary fly, and it was twice as stubborn. I could chase it to a corner of the room where it rested watchful and out of reach.

Her illness was terminal, Diabetic Cardiomyopathy (DCM). I knew I couldn't fight it. Hell, I could hardly chew on words so big. Only she could fight it. Fighting and losing was our current destination. I had taken a leave of absence that left me itching to return to my job. My career was the only thing that could eclipse the reality of my wife's pending death. The long, drawn-out process of saying good-bye was her lifeline, but it was killing me.

The marble kitchen counter was littered with tiny, toasted flakes of coconut. I liberated them with the tip of my pointer finger and placed them on my tongue. They were lost to the prior coconut, chocolate, and caramel that lingered on my tongue from before. I tried to steal back the lost moments, the never had moments, but the incessant buzzing returned in the wake of memories. Then I was purging in the sink to punish myself and assuage my guilt for living. In the silence of our cul-de-sac, I could hear the distant rush and bustle of suburbia. The sound of motion tapping on my windows. We needed new windows, but it would have to wait. The cough and rattle of rush hour mimicked the sound of Katrina's lungs. I needed a draught of Scotch to block the sound out of my ears. I put on my sound-canceling headphones, risking missing a call for help from Katrina, and I poured myself a drink. Shutting out what could be the last cries of her life. But I knew she wouldn't die like that, leaving me in peace. Katrina would grasp and clutch at me in the final throes of death, like a drowning victim taking her rescuer with her. The thought frightened me. I was afraid of death: hers and mine. I was scared of the invisible reach of a specter that would harvest my soul. I could not say any of this to Katrina, but I knew she could read it on my face.

Our wedding dresses hung at the back of our bedroom closet. Her's was heavy from the intricately beaded torso, and it had a long trail of buttons down the back. It took me forever to get her out of it while my simple white dress puddled around my feet on the floor. It had been an intimate wedding in our home, but still, she splurged on a gown that she never thought she'd get a chance to wear. We were in our early 40s when gay marriage was finally legal. There was enough space in the closet now to shuffle things about easily. My side had always been Spartan in comparison. Her side was packed tight. Once the closet bar collapsed under the weight of her winter wardrobe, but now it was thin. She'd instructed me to give away all the clothes for the summer season she wouldn't see and all the clothes that were now too big for her shrinking body. Katrina couldn't bear to look at them. Her fashion-forward days were over. She was not much more than a skeletal frame hung about with wasting flesh.

"What's wrong, Lulu?" she said.

I had stood in the doorway, watching her sleep, armed with my fly swatter. Now, she was awake. Katrina extended her arm and beckoned me. I stood at the foot of the bed with my head bowed like a shamed dog.

"I can't save you, and it's eating me up. There is nothing I can give or do to change our fate," I said.

"No one can. I was diabetic when we met. It wasn't a big deal. We ate healthily, and I took my insulin injections. There was nothing more to be done," Katrina said.

"I should have seen it coming," I said. "Gradually, you were tired all the time. Doing the laundry left you short of breath. Then on that Sunday morning, you fainted in the kitchen. Hitting your head on the marble counter, the frying pan fell to the floor and burned your thigh. I raced in at the sound of the sizzle and clatter. There was bacon everywhere. It was scattered on you and the floor. Your brow was bleeding profusely. You left your nightgown on the kitchen floor, and I helped you get dressed in your sweats; we went to the emergency room. We were so focused on the stitches, so stupid," I said.

We asked if we could see a cosmetic surgeon, but the medical staff was more interested in the mysterious fainting spell. We had chalked it up to a bad episode of diabetes. The ER doctor wanted to run some tests. When he returned, it was the first time I heard the term Diabetic Cardiomyopathy. Katrina was less surprised. Her father had died of heart failure due to DCM before we met. I was alarmed. I took Katrina home with her Frankenstein brow, and I got on the internet. I went straight to WebMD, and as always, that was a mistake. I now had enough information to scare the hell out of me but not enough to build a battle plan against.

After our first visit with the heart doctor, I felt worse; she felt worse. He'd said it was terminal, irreversible, and gave us a five-year sentence. I vowed to Katrina to be there for everything, and for the first two years, I was. Then the illness stretched its legs and moved about Katrina's body, causing manageable pain but dire circumstances. Like her weight and quitting smoking, the things we had control of were not enough to rein in DCM. The disease wanted more. It thinned the walls of her heart, which in turn enlarged the chambers. She was hopped up on pills: beta-blockers and ACE inhibitors. I was getting a crash course in pharmacology. She took drugs to ease the edema and drugs to help her sleep. I was given a script for Prozac. I thought about taking the whole bottle with a fifth of Jack. But I couldn't leave her. I returned to work part-time from home. Then I got a network of friends to babysit Katrina so I could go back to the office. It started off at 16 hours a week, and it quickly progressed to 40 hours in the office and more from home. Finally, hope came into our lives with a Left Ventricular Assist Device (LVAD) implanted to help her heart pump blood to the body. It was a stopgap while we sweat it out for a heart transplant. It never happened.

The harder I pushed away from Katrina's prolonged dance with death, the more difficult it was to return to her. I had expected I'd be holding her hand when the time came, but I wasn't. I was working on a new logo for a long-time client. A man that would come to Katrina's funeral to pay his respects. Respect I couldn't afford her in her passing. So, I renewed the script for the Prozac. The little orange bottle sat alone on the kitchen counter, and I eyed it warily with the shadow of a mound of pills inside. The pills were supposed to subdue the rage inside. They were supposed to help me build a ladder out of the pit of despair and guilt. I wondered how many it would take to heavily sedate me or maybe numb me out of existence. But even in my pain, I could not commit to ending my life. Death hurt, and I didn't want any more of it. I failed Katrina. She died in a hospital bed in the spare bedroom, alone. I was in the hall clutching a file to my chest, listening to the rattle of her breath. I imagined how her enlarged heart beating erratically must have caused her agony. I know listening to her life's exit caused me torment, but it didn't match the pain of my cowardice.

I stopped working. I started and stopped therapy. I never left the house. I got my scant groceries from Instacart. The hospital bed had been returned to a medical supply company. I sat in the empty space it left behind, my arms wrapped around my knees, rocking myself. I did not reassemble the full-sized four-poster bed that had been there. It was piled on the floor by the window like a shipwreck, a shambles. I slept in my office on the brown leather Chesterfield sofa. I could not go to our bed. I had not changed the sheets since she left them to take up residence in the spare bedroom. It was too much bed for me, alone. The wrinkled linens and divots still in place from her body haunted me. I felt sick to my stomach that I held on to her so tightly after she was gone, but I was scarce to be found when she needed me most.

At first, and for a while, I thought my depression was a tribute to her life. It was not. It was more cowardice. And like a reflection in a pond, the ripples shook my self-image. I was not the wife I'd thought I'd be. I could not face her dying, her death, nor my life. I was in limbo. I kept the Prozac filled, which meant I had to return to therapy. I lost my job. I had no insurance, so once again, I was without treatment and Prozac. I started cleaning. Dusting, sweeping, mopping, and finally, I removed the sheets from our bed and put them in the trash. I retrieved the red vacuum cleaner from the corner of the dining room. I hadn't vacuumed ever. She did that. I ran my hand over the handle. Katrina had taken one look at the shiny red Dyson vacuum when she unboxed it.

"I feel like the Mario Andretti of housewives," she said.

"You're not a housewife. You're an accountant," I said.

"I can pretend, can't I?"

"You can be anything you want to be," I told her.

I heard myself. I whispered it back. "You can be anything. I can be anything." I didn't have to be in pain. I could miss her and love her and move on in baby steps. I couldn't save her, but maybe, just maybe, I could save myself.

The Sound of Mischief

THE TIN MAN WAS WHEEZING. LUKE COULD hear him through the door of 6E. It was a laborious sound, a gasping, grasping at life sound. The sound of the Tin Man's assisted breathing had become a sound of comfort. When alone in his apartment, waiting for his mom, the silence built a timorous tower of anxiety. He turned the TV on for company, but he was compelled to watch the sensational *America's Most Wanted* religiously even though it scared the crap out of him. He was afraid to close his eyes lest a serial killer bust out of the kitchen. Because in Luke's mind, that is where killers reside, in kitchens with the knives. This anxiety pushed him out of doors and made him vulnerable to the bullies.

Luke stood on the landing longer than he should, listening. He was losing ground. Soon, Tyler and the other boys of the west side apartment building would find him, and then Luke would be sorry. He could hear their jeers growing in volume.

"Hey, Ass hat, We're going to find you," Tyler yelled.

The other boys laughed and repeated, "Ass hat, ass hat."

Luke still had a black eye, not even fading yet, from the other day when they found him by the recycling cans on the curb. Now, he heard the rapid trample of feet coming up the stairs, and he turned to flee to his apartment with the scuffed door from where the boys would kick and holler insults.

Luke should have stayed inside all day while his mother was at work, but looking out the window at the sun glinting off the cars, the birds hopping on the sidewalk at the edges of the trashcans, and the girls playing hopscotch, he was beckoned to play a part in the springtime city. Just a few weeks ago, snow and ice melted on the walk. Today, you'd never even know that winter had extended its reach trying to stake one final claim before the bursting warmth of spring hatched. The heat of the sun once more beat through the window, and Luke answered its call. He'd been outside unmolested by his bullies for 20 minutes. He checked his mother's old Swatch watch, the purple face too big on his wrist with a black mesh lace design. It was girly, but he wore it. And he liked to guess at the time. Of the moment, it was half-past a lace flower. He liked the watch. It made him feel closer to his mom. She worked long hours and sometimes weekends at an office that didn't pay enough for childcare. So, Luke was left alone for long periods, a difficult feat for an eight-year-old. Nevertheless, he endured the bullies, and his mother pretended to believe his stories of falling and bumping into things to get all of those bruises and black eyes. She had to believe him because she had no choice but to leave him behind.

The street was full of children's traffic that Monday of late May, and Luke sat in the window picking at a scab on his knee. Then, finally, the siren song of school released children, and the promise of summer to come coaxed Luke back out. Maybe this would be a good day when the boys would be mesmerized by Tyler's Xbox, and Luke could enjoy the breeze under the sun. But it was not; Luke was not out long when he heard the whistles and shouts of the small band of bullies. They were not much bigger than him, but they outnumbered him, and they were mean. Luke made a quick turn of it from the sidewalk and headed back to his apartment. The rhythmic sound of the old man breathing caught his attention on the landing between the Tin Man's apartment and his own; he paused and pressed his ear to the door. Luke wondered what the old man looked like and envisioned him as the Tin Man from the Wizard of Oz, wheezing, needing oil. Luke stepped back from the syncopated sound and quickly ascended the last flight of stairs.

ON SUNDAY, Luke saw no light seeping from under the Tin Man's door, just darkness. He stopped on his way back from the corner market to get milk and cereal for breakfast. He had a box of Lucky Charms hanging in a plastic bag from his left arm. He considered his mother still asleep upstairs, and then he got down on his stomach on the commercial-grade mottled brown carpet squares. Luke pulled at the edge of the carpet, using his fingertips, and he tried to sneak a peek under the door. Nothing. He listened to the sucking and pumping sound that broke the silence in the dark, ripping open life, forcing oxygen in and out of the Tin Man. Through the wooden door, the peeling paint, Luke could envision his Tin Man waiting.

———

ON WEDNESDAY, Tyler and the boys were hot on Luke's heels. Their summer camps had not yet begun. Luke was not going to make it to his door this time. He tripped up the stairs. His feet failing him in fear, and then he noticed the Tin Man's door ajar. Luke spontaneously and stealthily nudged the door open just enough for him to sneak his small body through the crack. The boys rumbled past while Luke waited just inside the door for the bullies to come back down the stairs in retreat, giving him the all-clear. As he waited, his eyes adjusted to the darkness, and he could hear them banging on the door to his empty apartment. Luke crouched in the pitch-black room. With time, he could even make out the silhouette of the Tin Man in bed, and he appeared to be sleeping. As he crept closer, he kept his steady gaze on the Tin Man's face. The Tin Man's eyes were closed. The room was stale and motionless, except for the pumping of the ventilator. He continued to step softly across the room to the old man elevated in a hospital bed. The bed and ventilator were centered in what should have been the living room.

Luke ran his fingers over the ventilator on a small side table. He was careful not to press any buttons. It was benign in shape and color, but Luke knew it kept the man alive despite its mundane appearance. Luke peered over the metal railing of the bed, taking in the domed plastic mask strapped to the old man's face. He wondered how the man could sleep like this. Luke once tried his mother's sleep mask, but he couldn't stand the pressure across his eyes. However uncomfortable, he figured the old man didn't have a choice. Then Luke noticed the flutter of the gray lashes. The Tin Man opened his eyes and turned a cloudy, fogged eye toward Luke. Luke fled the blind eye only to return hours later. The door was still hanging open as he left it when he raced home upstairs. He stepped into the broad shaft of light, partially blocking the illumination from the landing.

What light remained fell across the old man's face bloated with a pearly sheen. He was barrel-chested like the Tin Man. His right eye was cloudy, and he seemed to rely on his sense of sound and smell to navigate his small world. With a large, wrinkled, and meaty hand, he waived Luke in. As Luke crossed the room, he watched the Tin Man struggle to remove his ventilator. He fumbled and grasped with his fingers inside his mouth. Finally, he clutched and withdrew a wet tube with webs of saliva from the depths of his mouth and throat. This grotesque liberation was bound with the smell of foul breath. Luke's knees weakened, and he grasped the metal railing of the bed to steady himself while the Tin Man struggled with the mask and straps wrenching them from his face. The apparatus tumbled and dangled at his side. When the Tin Man parted his dry, cracked lips, a whispery, shaky voice shattered against the continual hush of the ventilator.

"Water," the Tin Man whispered.

Luke went to the neglected kitchen and fetched a glass of water. He felt the Tin Man was more like Darth Vader when Vader says, "I am your father." But Luke knew this elderly man was not his father. His father was across town and too busy to see him. The Tin Man was right here, and Luke suspected that they needed each other.

The Tin Man lived in a cave of shadows which Luke found comforting, like a blanket to hide under. Luke made garlic bologna and mayo sandwiches on white bread with the crust cut off to share with the Tin Man. As Luke ate and the Tin Man choked down his lunch, Luke told the Tin Man stories of the world outside. Eerily, the Tin Man knew the number of boys in the band of bullies. He could smell and name each one. Luke wondered what he smelled like.

"Fear, it is fear and Lucky Charms," the Tin Man said, and he coughed with a grimace of discomfort.

Luke could believe him. He often caught a whiff of sweat and Lucky Charms lifting off his body when hiding in a small space waiting for the boys to pass.

The Tin Man had good and bad days, and sometimes he dismissed Luke as soon as he entered. Other days, he told Luke horrific tales that kept Luke entranced in the darkness. The Tin Man spun breathy yarns of mischief and magic. And it was on a chill, wet afternoon that he told Luke about the Draugr.

"A Draugr is a powerful spirit that can possess the living and once occupying a body can shapeshift into another on contact. They are cruel creatures," the Tin Man said.

"Have you ever seen one?" Luke said.

"Oh, yes," the Tin Man said.

Luke wasn't certain, but he was inclined to believe the strained voice that strummed the air in the shadowy room.

———

IT WAS LATE IN THE DAY, on what otherwise would have been a beautiful Thursday. It was warmer than it had been in some weeks, and the promise of summer was beating down strong. Tyler had Luke pinned to the sidewalk, and he was raining down blows on him. Luke's skinny arms did nothing to protect his face. Tyler beat him savagely, and when he rocked back on his heels, hovering over Luke, to see what he had done, Tyler worried that he had gone too far. It was two weeks before Luke dared to leave the apartment, and when he did, he sprinted down to the Tin Man. He had forgotten how dark it was inside the Tin Man's home.

He hesitated to get his bearings. But all in all, Luke was thankful for the darkness. He was embarrassed for the Tin Man to see his shame.

"Let me see how bad," the Tin Man said.

"How did you know?" Luke said.

"Everyone knows," the Tin Man said.

The Tin Man gave him a once-over with his good eye.

"I think it's time," the Tin Man said.

"Time for what?" Luke asked.

"Revenge."

At first, their plots were fantastical and fun to imagine, but then things took a turn. The Tin Man was plotting something beyond mischief, something doable, something sinister. Unfortunately, Luke had a momentary lapse of judgment and played along with the Tin Man's fantasy of revenge. Initially, the plan seemed harmless. Luke was to lure Tyler into the Tin Man's apartment, and the Tin Man would scare him. While Luke doubted the Tin Man could scare someone like Tyler, he did like the idea of turning the tables.

"The next time we hear Tyler on the stairs below, you taunt him and run in here. Then, when he gives chase, you duck into the dark, and I'll let loose while you shut the door," the Tin Man said.

It was mere hours before they heard Tyler coming into the building. You could tell it was him because he was always singing the same song.

"Do your balls hang low? Do they wobble to and fro?"

"Hey, Ass hat," Luke shouted with glee.

Just like they'd planned, Tyler came barreling into the darkness. Luke slammed the door shut and leaned against it with his back to watch the show. Tyler was disoriented. The Tin Man was out of bed and slowly staggering forward. Luke and Tyler were both paralyzed in surprise. By now, Luke was used to the dark. He could see enough. The Tin Man lurched in his thin cotton pajamas. The pants were baggy, for they once fit a bigger version of the Tin Man. But through the threadbare shirt, Luke could see the Tin Man's frame. He had once been a hulking figure. Age had worn him soft and saggy. Crossing what looked like an impossible distance for a man in his condition, the Tin Man reached out and grabbed Tyler by the throat; as he tightened his grasp on Tyler's throat, he shifted, they changed. Bones cracked and collapsed to the floor. Bones snapped and built up a sturdy, albeit child's small stature. The flesh transaction was weepy and sticky. The Tin Man was shape shifting into Tyler, and Tyler was melting into an old man on the floor. The Tin Man gave a shudder as his new skeleton slipped into place, and his hunger was satiated. The new Tin Man Tyler stretched out his new arms, flexing and feeling their twiggy nature. He strolled toward Luke and gave him a hard stare.

"Come teach me about this Xbox," the Tin Man Tyler said, and he ushered the speechless Luke out the door.

We Were Just Visiting Life

WE THOUGHT WE WERE LIVING UNDER THE radar. Sometimes we knew we were hiding, glommed on to each other in our reclusiveness. No one went to college. No one had a job. But we had unraveled time; we had it by hours; we hoped for years. We had cigarettes, but I didn't even smoke. We had video games and inside jokes, locking the world out. A world that had already forgotten us. We had sex. Well, Royce and I had sex. It was the trapeze by which we clung and swung to life. None of us was ready to exit. No one could sing the swan song. At the bottom of society, overgrown children backing away from the cusp of adulthood, we held onto each other. But could we hold on tight enough? Life ignored us in turns when it wasn't gnawing on our bones with isolation.

It was always winter. It was always night. I know that can't be true, but that is what I feel when I look back. The cold snapping winds buffeted us between car and building and fit snug up against us during smoking rendezvous. Smoking was allowed inside Sean's house. Perhaps that is why his parent's home, Denny's, and Steak 'n Shake were our favorite haunts. We could just sit and smoke and talk at all hours. I don't think I'll ever meet such directionless people with so much to say, but maybe that's true of all youth. Clouds of smoke clung to our clothes, reeking, a constant halo of nicotine in my hair. Not my smoke; I didn't smoke. I just went along with everything. I breathed in the smoky exhalations, the poison of my friends.

I came to these people out of desperation. I arrived on the scene with my Winona Ryder haircut and heroin chic eye make-up. I was the newbie in the crowd. I'd been removed from DePauw before the end of my first semester. It was amazingly easy to accomplish. I stayed in my dorm room; I only left to use the bathroom. I thought college was going to knock me out of my unending ennui. I felt in the confines of a dormitory room, I would be forced to socialize. But my unnamed depression followed me from home. I thought if I failed to unpack the boxes piled under my lofted bed that I could keep the depression packed away, but I was wrong. Cardboard is not enough of a barrier to choke off the appetite of depression. The dullness and dispiritedness followed me to college. It hung about my shoulders like a weighted blanket. I never left my bed. I did not go to class. I did not party. I slept. I saw passing faces of curiosity, and I rolled over. Once I stopped bathing and using the restroom, my roommate had had enough. The one-use water bottles filled with urine were the deal-breaker. She ratted me out.

My parents came to fetch me. They said nothing. They hoisted the boxes, the ones they had unloaded just three months prior, back into their black Ford Explorer. I climbed into the back seat with my childhood blanket. It felt like coming to rest in a puffed-up hearse. I was hauled home the way other college students arrived with bags of dirty laundry. I passed the half-decorated Christmas tree, and I curled up in the cool sheets of my full-sized bed after dismissing our cocker spaniel, Lola. My geography and the holidays did nothing to improve my mood. But here, at home, I had parents to nag and demand I leave my bed, go out into the world. And I did.

The biggest problem of going out into the world was I had nowhere to go. I drove out of the subdivision in the big Bertha SUV and down the street to the QT. I didn't need gas. I cut the engine, which silenced the swoon and mourning sound of Morrissey. The car had still been warming up. I went inside and escaped the thick gray blanket of a January sky. I wanted a Coke slushy, but it was too cold for that. I decided on a hot chocolate and browsed the chips with the bland cocoa burning my left hand. There were boys in the next aisle. They were seemingly stocking up on beef jerky. One of the three rounded the end cap and came to a stop before me.

"Oh, sorry. What are you getting?" the boy said.

He had a grown-out Mohawk that dipped in his grey eyes. I gave him a blank look. My throat was constricted in anxiety, as I hadn't had much use for a voice in quite some time. I felt pinched in this situation.

I held out my bag of sour cream and onion Lays. His brow wrinkled, and he cocked his head to the right, the way Lola did when she didn't understand a command. But he was making an assessment. I waited under the fluorescent lighting.

"I like Fritos," he said, reaching for a bag.

I said nothing. I looked down at the toes of combat boots. I felt stupid as well as dumb.

"Well, I'll see ya," he said.

He checked out with his buddies. I had slinked back by the refrigerator case, all the while watching and sniffing his fading Drakkar Noir. To my dismay, he turned at the door to find me. And find me he did. He tossed off a wave and was gone. After this, I began making daily trips to QT. I always returned home with another bag of Lays and a pack of Twizzlers. I had given up on the hot cocoa.

"Sour Cream Lays?" he said.

His voice drifted over my shoulder. It startled me, but it shouldn't have as I had come here every day for two weeks looking for him. I was increasingly aware that I didn't really want to be alone.

"Um, no. Cheddar this time," I said.

I had spoken! It was the most outstanding achievement. He had no way of knowing what a breakthrough this was for me.

"Where are you going with those Lays?" he said, arching his eyebrows.

"Home," I said. There it was, my gift of gab gone already.

"Do you play Mortal Kombat?" he said.

"No. I know it. But I don't have a game system at home," I said.

"What? Really? What did you do?" he said.

"I failed out of DePauw. My mom boxed up the Sega," I said.

"Duh, what?" he said.

"DePauw. It's a college. I flunked out," I said.

I really didn't want to start with this, but he didn't seem to care.

"Oh, well. I'm going to my friend's house to play video games. Do you want to go with?" he said.

"The beef jerky guys you were with last time?" I said.

He coughed a little laugh, "Yeah, those guys."

"Okay," I said.

"But don't bring up the beef jerky. One of the guys is a vegetarian, so he's feeling bad about it," he said.

"Um, what's your name?" he said.

"Hailey. What's your name?" I said.

"Royce," he said. "Like a Rolls Royce, and just as sweet a ride," he said. It was definitely a practiced sound bite in his world.

I couldn't tell if he was mysterious or stupid.

Two months into my socialization, I still moved with lethargy, but now I listened to Nirvana. It was everything I could do to keep my depression at bay. It was my clinging to Royce that kept my head above water. Royce suggested I see someone, a therapist, a doctor, but he was all the outlet that I wanted. However,

I didn't want to drown him in my misery. I asked my mother to find me a shrink. She was not relieved as I had imagined but dismayed. Her own depression crept closer to the surface. I would have to do everything myself. My parents' insurance card was the beginning and end of their support for my mental health.

I could not find a line of demarcation for my depression. It was a gradual transition out of the bumbling lifestyle of adolescence into a gradual fade of existence. For all its slow positioning, it was unfathomable. I was zipped up in a body bag of blue funk. Royce was a peek-a-boo of light in my cave of existence, and he unfastened the deep-set underpinnings of my depression. He was just a fissure of light, but I was grabbing hold of that intangible shine. My gloom made it easy to fall in love with the radiance of Royce.

I had few friends in high school, and now they were gone off to different colleges learning and living, becoming real people. When they came home to visit and dump their laundry off on their mothers, I didn't have time for them, although I had all the time in the world. My world was made up of the boys, full stop. I wouldn't budge from them. People from my past were not worth the investment of a weekend. Perhaps, my hard line was due to the fact I never had a best friend until Royce. Someone who was there without fail. Someone I could trust. Why bother with the past on the periphery? Also, Royce was a miracle in my life. We were sleeping together, and I was at once vulnerable to and protected by Royce. I knew our relationship, as fresh as it was, teetered on his continued sobriety. From my post as a babysitter to his commitment to a clean and sober life, I could not spare a moment away from him. I quickly learned teetotaling was not feasible. So, an unspoken agreement to a recreational pursuit of alcohol and pot was the neutral zone. I would learn that just one of the flaws to this situation was that Royce had nothing but recreational time on his hands.

Sean's living room was a shabby hold-on to the 70s when we met. But I can hardly recall it because the house got a makeover three weeks into the friendship with new carpeting, even in the bathroom, which I found unclean. It was the kind of carpet that starts off matted down. The living room got an oversized, over-stuffed blue baby corduroy sectional sofa. The greasy dark brown wooden coffee table and matching end tables made the cut, somehow. Sean's mother rightly knew we'd forget to use coasters for our fast-food sodas. No point in buying something just to have it ruined.

We all stood huddled on the front porch under a roof of snow and icicles dripping just two feet away. Royce and I smelled of sex; all of us smelled of cigarettes. The smells clung tight to us. Sean's chest of drawers and a bed frame crowded around us. The furniture had been moved out front while the men worked. The stacked drawers, liberated from the chest, put Sean's clothes on display. I was wrist-deep in his sock drawer with a menthol cigarette between my lips. I was trying smoking, so I hadn't bought my own yet. I was sampling off of the boys. Sean smoked the menthols, and he could exhale from his mouth and inhale through his nose. It was called a French Inhale. His long blond hair swept forward like a veil and hid his sly lips. I wanted to learn how to French Inhale. Royce and Fox smoked Camels in a hard box. After two weeks, I was still trying to figure out how to do a regular inhale. The boys were discussing setting up the basement for our use. A decade ago, Sean's older brother lived down there when he got his girlfriend pregnant, and she became his wife. They and their kid were years gone. The Black Sabbath poster still clung to the wall. Sean, Fox, and Royce were concocting a plan to makeover that shag rug, queen-sized waterbed room into a living room.

"We can haul some chairs out of the storage section. And I bet my mom will let us have the old sofa," Sean said with ramped-up excitement. He pushed his sleeves up like he was preparing to lift something.

I kept digging in the sock drawer, wondering where he kept his underwear.

"My Dad's got an old TV in our basement. My Mom's always after him to get rid of it," Fox said.

"Shit! That thing's going to be really heavy, "Sean said.

"Do you have a better option," Fox said.

"We can do it. And I'll donate my old system," Royce said. "It's a Sega Genesis."

"This is going to be wicked," Sean said.

Within a week, we were corralled by dated furniture on one side of an unfinished wall in the basement's bellows playing Sega NHL '95. The other side of the studded-out wall housed a floor-to-ceiling mash-up of junk. Mostly, I just sat in Royce's lap and watched, but sometimes I got in the way of his gaming action and had to move to the waterbed. The room was crammed with guitars, guitar amps, folding chairs, a space heater, and a black light. Already, trash was collecting on the floor newly carpeted with the old carpet from upstairs. We were perpetrators, lazy collectors of a trash-driven culture, and we, too, were victims of this throwaway society. Four kids/adults tossed aside and taking up space. There was an exit to the backyard. The window of the door was hung with a green and yellow lion's headscarf. We couldn't use the door because there was no lock, but the door had swelled shut. We couldn't break the seal. All three of the boys were in a state of recline with their black Vans propped up on the furniture, except Sean he was barefoot as usual. My combat boots were slumped against the waterbed where I sat curled up in an electric blanket. It was cold in the basement.

"So, why did you guys drop out of school?" I asked. I knew Royce had dropped out over too much time in drug rehab.

"I don't know. Why'd we drop out, Fox?" Sean said.

"Well, Royce was out, and it was wasting our time," Fox said.

"Ah, okay," I said with judgment.

"Well, smarty-pants, why did you drop out of Duh Paw?"

"I didn't. I flunked out, ha," I said.

"Yeah, Sean. Failing and dropping are totally different," Royce said with a chuckle mocking Sean and me.

At least I made it to college, I thought. But I kept that comment to myself.

"So, what have you accomplished with all your free time?" I begged of Sean.

"We beat Mortal Kombat," he said.

It was the end of the conversation. But it felt like everyone was harboring thoughts after this.

I was stretched out on the waterbed. Sean had just flipped the black light on. And what was revealed made me lose my appetite for my Steak n Shake cheeseburger with everything. That room looked like a porno horror movie under black light. I moved into Royce's lap. The only clean place to sit. Even Sean and Fox were limited in the number of jokes they could crack. Sean shut off the black light, and we tried to move on to a different topic. I grabbed a printout of the Purity Test out of my purse, and I began reciting the questions to the room.

"Have you ever masturbated?" All three boys thrust their hands in the air with pride.

"Okay, that's a resounding yes," I said.

"Have you ever used drugs to lower someone's sexual inhibitions?" I asked.

"Wait," Fox protested. He flipped his grown-out mullet over his shoulder with a toss of his head. "You didn't answer the last question."

"I'm not taking the test. I'm reading it," I said.

"Bullshit," Fox said.

"Leave her alone," Royce said.

"No, she has to take it just like the rest of us," Sean piped in.

"Okay, okay, Yes," I said sheepishly to the boys' hoots and hollers.

"Next question?" I said. "Have you ever used drugs to lower someone's sexual inhibitions?"

All three boys answered no.

"Have you ever masturbated into a house plant?"

"What?" Sean said.

"I'm not rereading it," I said.

"Who on earth has done that? And why?" Sean said.

We were all in agreement that was a crazy question. I moved on.

"Have you ever committed a crime?" I said.

Sean and Fox said no. Royce said yes.

"Every time I get high, I am breaking the law. When I got caught and put in rehab, it was because I broke the law," Royce said defensively. "Besides, Fox, I think you need to change your answer."

"Why?" I asked.

"Yeah, you do," Sean said.

Fox mumbled something. It was the first time I saw him crumble under peer pressure.

"Yes," he said, speaking more clearly.

"What was it?" I asked.

"He was nabbed for shoplifting," Sean said.

"What did you steal?" I asked.

"A stupid troll doll," he said.

"Make it five stupid troll dolls, the big ones like Cabbage Patch kids," Sean said, laughing.

"I don't understand," I said with a giggle.

"Look, I was only going to steal one troll doll, but it was so easy I went for five," he said.

"Why?" I said.

"I thought I could sell them. But I was bulging conspicuously, and I was caught by a mall cop," Fox said.

"You couldn't outrun a mall cop?" I said.

"The dolls were too bulky," Fox said.

"So, what happened?" I asked.

"My parents got a lawyer. I had to go to court and do community service," Fox said.

"Well, where the hell were you?" I asked Sean.

"I was home with strep throat," he said.

"Go to the next question," Royce said.

"Have you ever seen a stripper?" I said.

They were all talked out. The "No" framed in their minds seemed to take the steam out of the Purity Test engine. I tossed it to the floor and watched more of the mind-numbing NHL '95 video game. I set to braiding Royce's hair to keep myself entertained.

Sean and Fox were close, while Royce had been the third wheel. Sean and Fox had been friends their whole lives and did everything together. They'd played little league together, trick-or-treating together, learned to drive a car together under Sean's older brother Billy's instruction. They did everything together, including dropping out of high school. It was not a well-thought-out plan for the long run. So, their mothers made sure they took the GED together. And life settled into the routine as I knew it. When I watched them, it was pretty evident that Sean was home base. All life was lived in his house. I'd never even been to Fox's house. I knew right where it was, just five doors around the corner. While Sean was liege over our hangout, Fox was the leading personality in the group. He was the most outgoing. He came up with the ideas when it was time to change the venue to Denny's or Steak n Shake. Fox was the one to select the movies at Blockbuster Video. Fox generally picked the fast food. Royce was on-trend. He always had the latest and greatest of games, fashion, food, what have you. Royce had the pool. Not that I had a chance to try it out yet, with it only being March.

We couldn't be bothered with things like umbrellas. The boys were all wearing long black leather trench coats, an essential garment of our age. I stood inside Royce's coat, my forehead pressed against his chest, a sanctuary from the wet. The car took too long to warm up and defrost the windshield. Little clouds of clarity crept up, creating tiny windows in the ice. I slumped in the driver's seat to see out these pockets. It was the middle of the night, and winter held spring in its clutches. But I was in a subdivision I knew well. As long as I could make out the parked cars dotting the outlines of the road, I could make it home. We kissed goodnight, and I drove to my subdivision. We would repeat it all tomorrow. Winter begrudgingly passed into spring, but we never changed. The leather coats were eventually stored in closets.

Fox had declared a celebration and planned the whole thing. We would meet up on the top of Cliff Cave trail. Sean was in charge of salty snacks, and I was in charge of sweets. And to my chagrin, Royce was in charge of the pot. The celebration was on a late spring night at the beginning of May, the kind of night that gets chilly with the evening's waning, but the day had been one of blue skies and promise. When Royce showed up to get me in his mom's grey accord, he'd brought tulips. They looked worn. He said the petals had been pinched for luck, pinched by him. I inspected the bruised petals and wondered if pinching tulips was really a thing. It looked far more likely they had belonged to his mother for several days already. I was getting recycled flowers. It didn't matter. None of us had any money. I set the vase of tulips on the dining room table where they could begin their second life. I pinched a petal for good measure and then followed Royce out the door.

Fox had built a small fire. I thought it a little too close to the edge, but Fox danced around to demonstrate safety. His boom box was seated a safe distance from the heat of the fire and played Peter Gabriel. Sean had brought little wieners to roast on skewers from his mother's kitchen. I had got the marshmallow, graham crackers, and Hershey's chocolate bars. I didn't think of skewers, so we had to find sticks to avoid cross-contamination between the wieners and the marshmallow. Royce sat to my right side, leaning toward the dancing flames to get enough light to roll a joint. I was a marijuana virgin, but I wanted to be able to participate this night. However, I still wasn't great at inhaling. I didn't understand why it was so hard for me. It made me feel stupid. I mean, if the guys could do it, I should be able to do it. I sat on a log next to Royce, who was already smoking. Finally, after a couple of passes around the circle, it began to hit me. Everything was slow and funny. I felt dazed and hyper-focused. The mix of wieners, beer, marshmallows, and weed made a heady perfumed fog about my head and in my mouth. It didn't seem so bad.

Sean's dad drank Bud Light, so we drank Bud Light. It did the trick, but I'd rather have snagged a bottle of my Mom's Riesling, except she would have noticed. The darkness felt like it was encroaching on our revelry, an uninvited guest. I cuddled up with Royce and knocked his marshmallow off his stick in the process. He reached in the bag for a new one and gave me a kiss. Fox was talking, but I wasn't paying attention. I had locked in on the smear of marshmallow and chocolate on my navy-blue tights. It was right across the top of my knee. I wasn't sure how it got there. Was it marshmallow or a tear revealing a pucker of my white flesh?

"I have an announcement to make. I'm going to college," Fox shouted. He was standing with his arms outstretched while we remained seated. Everyone was silent. "It's not Duh Paw," Fox said and laughed.

"That's great. Remember to get out of bed and actually go to class," I said, putting in my words of wisdom.

"Cool, Dude. Where?" Royce said.

"Mizzou," Fox said, feeling proud.

"How?" Sean said.

"I sent my records. I got in. My parents are thrilled," Fox said.

"Why didn't you tell me?" Sean said.

"I don't know. I didn't think you'd be into it," Fox said.

"But we do everything together. Everything," Sean said.

His jaw was growing tighter with every word he spoke. I held the roach out to him, but he was oblivious.

"Look, Dude. I know you didn't pass the GED. You never got the certificate in the mail. Your Mom would have hung it on the wall," Fox said.

"Fine, just fine," Sean said.

Fox sat back down. He was still feeling great from the beer, pot, and his accomplishment. He couldn't hide the grin on his face. The circle fell silent except for Metallica now playing on the mixtape in the boom box. I reversed and handed the roach back to Royce. It began its circuit in the opposite direction. I was not sure if we sat in stillness and quiet for a long time or not. My perception of time was warped.

Sean pulled a revolver out of his backpack and put it in his lap. We were a captive audience. I couldn't tell you what kind of gun it was. I knew nothing about guns, but it certainly had my full attention. I liked the way the flicker of the campfire danced across the barrel.

"What the hell, Dude?" Fox said.

"Let's play a game," Sean said. Every word dripped with defiance.

"Why did you bring that?" Royce asked.

"I thought we could shoot the cans," Sean said.

"With a revolver?" Royce said.

"Shall I put up the cans somewhere," Fox said.

"But now, come to think of it, I have a better game," Sean said and loaded one bullet in a chamber. He spun it and locked it in place.

"Russian roulette," Sean said.

"Are you crazy?" I said. Royce wrapped me up tight in his arms.

"Are you scared?" Sean said.

He held the gun to his head.

"Wait," Fox said. "I'll go first."

Fox stood up and took the revolver out of Sean's hand. He passed it back and forth between his hands as if weighing the heaviness of the gun. I averted my eyes. Then he held it to his right temple. Without warning, Sean dove at him.

"No! I didn't mean it," Sean yelled.

Sean was positioned to hit Fox with all his weight, but Fox dodged out of instinct.

Sean was gone. Just like that. He was over the cliff edge with a scream. Royce and I screamed. Fox dropped the gun and looked over the edge.

"Shit! Sean, Sean, Sean. Can you hear me?" Fox screamed.

Royce and I scrambled to Fox's side. We lay in the dirt on our stomachs listening and looking, but we could see nothing in the dark. Fox removed a flashlight from his backpack. He shined the light down the sheared-off cliff. We could just make out Sean at the bottom. My vision was turbid and bloated.

"We have to go down there," I said. My statement felt long and drawn out.

"We can't climb down in the dark," said Fox.

"We will go back to the car and drive around," Royce said.

"We can't. You can't," Fox said. "If we get caught with the beer, pot, and gun? Dude, you are on probation."

Royce fell silent. He backed up a few paces.

"I'd go to jail. I'm not serving time for this," Royce said. "I can't get into trouble again. I can't be found breaking the law because I already broke the law."

"Fine. You go home. Fox and I will handle it. Sean needs medical attention," I said.

"Hailey, I think Sean is dead," Fox said. "Look at this drop-off. And he's not answering us."

I peered over the edge into the night. I worried about falling off myself, about being dead with Sean at the bottom. I imagined myself busted open on the rocks. I scuttled back from the edge. I was good at taking things too far and falling over a precipice. Did I move just in time? Was I ever in danger? I stood a good three feet back from the bluff for a long time, I think. I was in a spiral of doubt. I looked up at the stars. They were faint in the ambient light, and I wished it were darker or they were brighter. I stared into the vaulted ceiling of our campout, gasping for air. I couldn't look down anymore. Nirvana's "No, I Don't Have a Gun" was playing a little too loud. It had been playing when Sean fell. How could it still be playing? Was it on repeat? The chilled wind rattled the trees and my bones. It made a swishing sound that mixed with the crackling fire and plaintive, dead Kurt Cobain. I could have listened to it all night long. As horrible as it was, I didn't want to leave that moment. I didn't want to face reality.

"I can't get caught like this either. This and the shoplifting offense on my record? I can kiss Mizzou goodbye," Fox said.

"Now you are worried about Mizzou? A moment ago, you were going to shoot yourself in the head," I said.

Fox opened his hand; the bullet was there.

"I took it out," Fox said. "I didn't want to play Russian Roulette. I was calling Sean's bluff."

I looked into their shadowy faces distorted by firelight and substance. I couldn't decide if they were cowards or pragmatic. And then, I let Royce lead me away. I let me follow.

It was the end of the summer. We had all been suspects and were interrogated by the police. Sean's mother begged us for answers. We left her with the emptiness of the unknown. Our secret was sealed with a panicked promise to each other, but the secret bust the seams of our friendship, whereas I thought it would strengthen our attachment. We couldn't keep it together, so we had to keep it apart. Fox got what he wanted. He went to Mizzou. Royce escaped on a road of drugs. His excursions led him to heroin, and he slipped between my fingers. I sank deeper into my depression. My social outlet was my weekly visits to my therapist. Only Fox survived. The rest of us died that night, even if we didn't know it at the time. We had not yet lived. We were just visiting life. And now we'd never know life without its companion, death.

Hello, Laura

I KEEP YOU IN MY CONTACTS. I VISIT YOU ON voicemail and short video messages. The pulse of electronica doses the air from Google's playlist of 80s nostalgia, and I'm scratching the itch to get back to you. We're in front of your white wicker framed mirror in the bedroom you shared with your older sister, whom I have put on a pedestal, but you haven't. When I look at you, hope and promise bubble up from my sweaty toes to burp games of our concoction. You are confident. You teach me how to ride a bike with finesse. You set me on the banana seat of your Schwinn and spin me around the cul-de-sac. You cheer me on. I keep pedaling, afraid to stop. I don't want to fail in front of you. It had to be boring, but you seemed satisfied to teach. I am impressed by you.

When we were 16, we lay on our bellies, side-by-side on your sister's bedroom floor, flipping through a playgirl magazine. The air is charged with glossy pages of sex. I'd never seen a penis before, and I'm not sure if I'm excited or disappointed. Those must be good ones if they are in a magazine. We giggle and put everything back under your sister's bed.

Then we turned 21 and danced like Bowie. Just like the days in your white wicker framed mirror when we developed second-grade dance moves to the Go-Go's, Adam Ant, and ABBA. But now, your signature move is an outstretched arm, palm up, pushing back the sneak-up humper. You were the keeper of the sanctity of the booty. You always knew who was a keeper and who needed to be banished. We started drinking at my house, vodkaritas, an invention of my little brother to save money. He didn't drink them; he just mixed. We had traded our jumpsuits for slip dresses and high heels. Time slips away, and we have to reach out to find each other again. I wonder how life ebbs and flows, but the calling card of history bridges every gap. I'm grateful for time's cyclical rubbing of our lives.

Mommy to mommy, we trade domestic war stories, laughing over bricks of Rice Krispy treats. You walk to your car in the early winter drizzle. My eyes follow you. God, I love that wool Kelly-green coat of yours. One day I find I do not want all you have. You call me and tell me you found a lump. It is as large as the one in my throat. But I can swallow mine away. What are you going to do? You fight; of course, you do. You throw a pink-themed Bye-Bye Booby party. You are a princess and a superstar with your boa and tiara. If no one knew, they'd be dying to be you. A full-frontal assault is your plan of attack. Everyone rallies behind you.

You get tired a year later, but you, little toy soldier, will never give up the fight. Your young daughter shampoos the sprinkles on your head, the stubby re-growth. Each bath time tugs on your heart, and with the ache, a little more of your history sloughs off. I don't know how to help you capture those giggles that felt invincible back in the day. I get busy. I fade into the false hope of tomorrow. For the first time, I don't know what to say to you. I feel let down by yesterday, and in the present, I'm wading in the shoals of death. I'm knee-deep in your family's dirty laundry: wash, dry, fold, repeat. This simple task is what I can do for you.

We're not even old enough to have wills. I trace my memories. Standing on the threshold of your living room behind your dad's recliner, quietly watching Star Trek. I'd never seen it before. Your mother's casseroles were eye-opening compared to our endless parade of pasta. There were co-birthdays, slumber parties, sleeping to the radio tuned to KHTR, Girl Scouts badges that mean nothing now, just tagging us growing up. In mischief and prayer, we are bonded. We walked down the aisle together for our first communion, conjoined and small. The roll of thunderstorms blows in. You hated each one, a potential home-wrenching tornado. I loved them like the gruff rumble and gravel of the grandpa who never gave up cigarettes.

"Hello, Laura let me know when you have some time to get together."

"Hello, Laura. Can I help?"

"Hello, Laura."

How To Make Waffles Like Mom

I AM A BULLY WITH AN ORIGIN STORY. I DON'T really have a type of victim. The closest I'd be able to label it was someone vulnerable. I measure my misanthropic manifestations as minor mishaps, misdeeds of meanness, such as helping an old woman carry her groceries to her car and bluntly making off with a bag or two. However, I didn't enjoy my ne're do well moments. It's just that assuming the bully's role was a more natural way to access my mother, who died two years back. Over the mortality divide, I tried to force a confrontation and put this trauma to bed and my mother to rest. Granted, she was six feet under in Sweetgum cemetery with a sizable granite tombstone. It stated her name and that she was a mother, and then dates of here and gone. It said something about being beloved, which one of my sisters put in. Sally, Mary, and Catherine had a different mother than I did. They had a beloved mother. I had the accursed, set upon, put out mother. My mother was plagued with the son of a bastard, who had walked out when I was four. I had become her albatross by the time I was five. She had no need of men, she'd say. And she sure as shit was not going to raise a womanizing little dick like him.

To be honest, it was my own fault the first time. Mom was curling sally's ponytail for school, and I was eating a piece of grape jelly toast.

"Get that toast out of here, Jacob," Mom said. "You're going to get jelly all over the bathroom."

"Yeah, Jacob, you're going to get jelly all over," Sally parroted Mom. That was her only talent to repeat Mom. For most of our childhood, I hated her. I didn't need two Moms walking around, fingering my real and unreal transgressions. Even when Sally knew the Lego mess was hers or the deck of cards on the coffee table, an abandoned, failing game of solitaire, Sally had no compunction of letting me take the wrath of being a slouch and weak. Sally's transgressions were pinned on me, and as Mom's attention magnified with each unforgivable sin, I was getting more and more of her attention. So, while I was pushing my luck with the jelly toast, I saw the opportunity to engage with Mom, and maybe gain something more than wrath, like sympathy, God, what I wouldn't have given for some sympathy from her punched-up curled lips.

Mom set the curling iron on the gold-flecked sink counter. I dropped my toast on the bath rug, a slight flaking of crumbs with a blob of grape jelly on the white bathroom rug. Mom and Sally turned toward the purple glob of horror, and I wrapped my hands around the curling iron barrel. The sound of my own scream was surprising to me. I had really no idea how bad that was going to hurt, and hours later, how bad it would keep burning. My sisters caught the bus, although Sally wanted to stay back and put her two cents in. I shored up any notions that men have a lick of sense in them for Mom. After that day, I was her testament to the stupidity of men and boys. I wondered if I hastened my place of lowliness in her eyes. If I had been brave enough to go out for the baseball team, the swim team, any team, I might have won her approval. But those dreams were spent in the bathroom that morning. I was a worthless fool.

—

THE SECOND TIME, and every time after that, Mom was the guilty one with the curling iron. My sisters would be in the living room, watching, dumbfounded by the morning cartoons and commercials. Then, if it was a school morning, Mom would hurry to corral my sisters out the door and to the bus stop. As soon as they were made scarce, Mom would do it.

"Hold your hand out. Palm up," Mom said.

In the beginning, my palm would bead up with sweat in anticipation of the coming burn. If I screamed, Mom would break out in her own sweat against her brow, followed by a slow creep of a smile on her face. When she removed the iron, the first thing she did was check her curling iron for flesh. Then she'd admire her handiwork. Next was the forgiveness I was giving her. I would make little coos as she cleaned and dressed my left hand. At that moment, she was motherly. Her voice was also soft like a nesting pigeon. Then she would drive me to Sweetgum Elementary school.

⁓

ONCE THIS RITUAL was tacked in our home, it was just a matter of time before school wondered about my bandages and scars. Mom received a phone call and had to pay a visit to the principal's office. I had no idea the power of the principal reached all the way back home. The next day, I walked in to class, bearing hard looks from my mother. She sat in the sitting area of the principal's office; she tapped the heel of her left mustard pump in a rapid rat-a-tat-tat. Even the dust bunnies shirked her presence. By the time my sisters and I tumbled through the front door, I wished I could blend in with them: curls, ribbons, and giggles. But I stood out as I always did.

"Jacob, come in here, please," Mom said.

I met her in the bathroom.

"Put your hand out," she said.

She'd never burned me in the evening, only right after breakfast. It hurt the same, but my stomach felt empty, knowing I was vulnerable to her any time. But in the evening, she'd have less time to care for me. There was dinner to get on and laundry to do. Mom told me the story she gave the school. I was informed I was to play along. And I did; it made us complicit in something. It was something I could give her, and she'd be forced to give it back.

Mom had told Principal Sallow that she was worried about me, that I was different. How she'd repeatedly warned me not to touch the curling hour, but inevitably I would. She was thinking of seeking out a child psychiatrist. Principal Sallow gave my mom a referral, someone in the school system. Mom accepted the business card, and I watched her throw it in the white bathroom waste bin. Mom held no truck with that mental crap.

———

THE FOLLOWING SCHOOL YEAR, I lucked out and got Miss Wisse for fifth grade. She was a billow of logic against the storm front of my mother. For every obvious answer my mother gave, Miss Wisse had another interrogation. In the second semester, over Easter breakfast, my sisters, too old to participate in egg hunts, were next door at the Smiths, helping the little kids and helping themselves.

Mom was making a stack of waffles. I was foolishly nearby.

Mom had filled the iron with batter and paused to look at me.

"You're getting big," she said. "You've grown a good four inches this school year."

I watched her watching me. By this point, I knew her look of interest could only simmer down into my injury.

"Put your hand in the waffle iron."

I hesitated, and she grabbed me by the wrist to force my hand. As she closed the iron, I considered that the batter might buffer the burn, but my hand's overall damage would be increased.

Upon release from the waffle iron, it was apparent that it actually was less damaging than gripping a curling iron. A sense of relief nestled briefly in my grasp. Mom removed the half-cooked, half flesh fragmented waffle and settled it on my plate. She looked like she'd just swallowed a prize kill. A new form of torture had been served up. When Easter break was over, Miss Wisse was on watch for me. She inquired about my burn's real estate, and I told her it was a waffle iron. Mom was already on the phone with the school secretary, telling our sad tale. In the end, Miss Wisse, as well-meaning as she was, was no match for my mom. I felt a little bit proud.

TO THIS DAY, I cannot eat waffles. I think that must be a normal reaction, as is my weakness to torment and intimidate women and little girls with ribbons in their hair. Each pass of my scarred hand across their smooth and shapely limbs reinforces my monstrosity. But there are no amount of vulgar passes that can win back my innocence or the loss of my mother. With each probe of my foul hand clutching and cutting off a clump of hair, I fail to own my victims; as mother possessed me, hair is not flesh. I sink further from my mother because it is not the same. I cannot make my victims love me. I cannot make them complicit in horror. There is a hole inside me widening, growing more profound.

In the end, all I have is a collection of lank hair that cannot excise my demons nor fill this hole. So, I stand alone with my left hand's deformity compelled to invoke revulsion. And I am called by my mother's burning love, which has made for a wildfire of itching scars that will not yield forgiveness for either one of us.

Stained Sheets

WHEN MY DAUGHTER WAS LITTLE, EVERY sheet set, duvet, curtain, lamp, and stick of furniture was carefully selected, curated to her tastes as they fell inside Pottery Barn's universe. The thread count, the ruffled trim, the color scheme was high-end quality chic, including the handcrafted chandelier. Then a few years piled on, and the divorce. We fought over everything. The house was sold to another family, and our family was broken. We were no more. We were not worthy of that house. It ousted us and held its charms for people who were worthy of comfort. We were shrugged off like a wet blanket of snow from the eves. The house displayed its riches for those making new memories.

My memories were packed in boxes. My ex hadn't wanted the photos, frames, and scrapbooks—the asshole. But I was glad because I needed it all. My proof that we had once been privileged by love. Instinct made me cling to material items like blankets and sheets. I was angry when handing over her Pottery Barn bedding to him, but they would not go with the mint green room I had for her now. A small room with a rattling window. The chandelier I'd gotten on Etsy was left behind. The ceiling of the duplex was too low, anyway. This was how I built a new life in mismatched, used blocks. Goodwill, where once I donated decor and clothes gathered in trash bags with the seasons' change, was now a place I shopped. One income and child support did not meet our accustomed needs. The divorce was not just a divide of a marriage, but it was the breaking of lives. The only one who knew what I was going through was standing on the other side of the divide.

My daughter slept on a bare mattress for the first month. My depression kept me from furnishing the basics of home. It was a weekend with her father when I hauled my ass out of bed. I drove to the Goodwill in my sweats. The whole store smelled of wasted dreams. The bed linens were tucked away in a corner with worn-out wreaths and chipped plates. There in a pile, second from the top, was a pink unicorn flat sheet, just like the one she had before the lilac butterflies. Were these hers? I snatched up the sheet. I stretched it out, looking for the puke stain in the corner. It was red Gatorade. All my efforts to clean it had faded it to dark pink. It wasn't good enough. So, I replaced it. Now, here it was. This was it. I sniffed it, and the Downy Fresh Unstoppables scent clung to the fabric. I began digging through the other piles knocking things askew. The fitted sheet was missing. Who only buys a fitted sheet? Here I was in flip flops and sweats, crying into the stained unicorn sheet, wiping away at my snot.

There was a woman at my elbow.

"Can I help?" she said.

"What?" I said.

"What are we looking for?" she said.

"The fitted sheet. The unicorn fitted sheet in pink," I said.

I couldn't express my thanks, but I was sure I was wearing my desperation on my face like a hangover. I gripped the stained unicorn sheet to my chest and zealously dug through poorly folded sheets with my other hand. There it was. Weren't these sheets just material things? But clutched in my hand, they were so much more. They were broken promises, a life unloved, a high thread count of security; they were mine. And now I would pay pennies on the dollar for my old, stained life. How much more would I pay to have it all back? But I wouldn't because it was a lie. These sheets were my past, which I dragged with me as I backed up a step away from the table. Wandering through my mind, I'd been unwilling to acknowledge the past was stained and had been for quite a while. Did I want to carry that forward? I looked down at the little unicorns. I didn't want to launder them again. Stretch them across the mattress again. I folded both sheets and put them back together in the stack, making some effort to rebuild. I wouldn't get mired in the wreckage of my marriage. I'd go buy some sheets at Target.

Spooning

L ILLIAN AND MARVIN WERE MARRIED FOR 35 fruitless years.

"It's not like nowadays where women take drugs like cocktails and viola, twins or triplets or, heaven forbid, more," Lillian bemoaned to Stan in June.

"In the '70s, you still did things the old fashion way; by time fertility clinics came on the scene, Marvin said we were too settled in our ways to add kids to the picture. Now, he's married to a 25-year-old baby with a baby on the way." That was September.

"Here I am, all alone with a mortgage and a leaky roof. Nature cheated me of children. And then Marvin cheated with a woman young enough to be our child." That was October.

But moreover, where did the love go? This question plagued Lillian as she unloaded the dishwasher, folded the reduced laundry, looked in the mirror, and drove to the appointments with Stan.

Lillian kicked off her favorite heels, the taupe ones with the well-worn creases where the foot flexed. She nudged them under the kitchen table with her feet. Unbuttoning her cardigan with one hand, Lillian opened the freezer with the other. She grasped the carton of vanilla ice cream and set it on the counter while she fished out her favorite spoon. It was the one that didn't match her set. She didn't know where it came from. It just appeared one day. If she flipped the spoon over, the ladle fit perfectly in the roof of her mouth. It was smooth, not scarred by an accidental spin in the garbage disposal. The handle was well balanced, and it had a simple beaded design along the edge. It was pleasing, arousing. The spoon's weight felt better in her hand, more luxurious than the other spoons, which felt flimsy, cheap, and temporary. Lillian found her spoon and stuck it upside down in her mouth for a sensual fullness to fill the empty space. She pried the lid off the ice cream and peered inside at the slick bottom of the carton with a lone scoop of vanilla.

"Shit, now I have to go back out," she said to no one.

It's 6:00 p.m. I'm going to have to drive in the dark. Marvin always drove for me at night. If I get jumped in the parking lot, it will be all his fault.

Lillian looked back inside the empty ice cream carton and resolved to brave the grocery parking lot. She put her heels back on, slipped into her beige wool coat, and scurried out the door.

Under a fluorescent gleam, Lillian selected a cart free of trash and Kleenex and placed her large leather purse in the seat section of the cart, the part meant for a small child. She thrust her gloves inside, and a whiff of Big Red gum puffed out like a punch of stale cinnamon. The smell of an old lady's purse.

Hmm, I might as well get a few things while I'm here.

At an even pace, Lillian clicked and creaked up and down the aisles. She surveyed the jams and preserves before choosing a squat jar of Orange Marmalade from the top shelf. Lillian turned to walk away but felt a slight tug at her left calf. Her pantyhose were snagged on a coupon offer flagged on a lower shelf. She pulled at the thread and freed herself to reveal a pale lump of flesh, filling the hole like a gagged mouth. Lillian picked up her pace to Frozen Foods and stood with her legs crossed in a manner that could be called coy but was intended to hide her small naked mistake. She opened the freezer door and grabbed a carton of Edy's vanilla ice cream tucking it under her arm, then grabbed a second one. Both containers are dumped into the cart, and she hastens toward the checkout.

A line? A line at this hour? Come on.

Lillian peeked over at the self-service checkout. Lillian hated self-checkout. She didn't pay these prices to do the work herself.

Third, in line, she waited. The man's sour breath behind her moistened the back of her neck and creeped around to her nostrils.

Why does he have to stand so close? Why does he have to breathe like that?

Lillian edged up to the magazine rack to escape the mouth breather. The tabloid headlines of broken Hollywood marriages begged, "What Went Wrong?" And she was pitched back to her grinding train of thought.

Where did it go? Where? I'm not a Hollywood starlet; besides, my marriage would have been a success in Hollywood terms. The love didn't die. I would have felt that.

The line advances. "Paper or plastic?"

"Paper." Lillian placed the last, already soft carton of ice cream on the conveyor belt. A small dribble of vanilla cream leaked from the lid and puddled in the web of flesh between her finger and thumb. It dripped onto the inside sleeve of her beige wool coat. She wanted to grab the checker, the bagger, the man behind her with his heavy sighs, and scream at all of them.

Where did it go? Where?

But she didn't. She wouldn't. She knew the love was simply left behind. It was with her. It was in her spreading hips and drooping jowls. The love didn't go. She could taste it, vanilla. It had just grown bland and old.

Shush

PENNIE STOOD NEXT TO HER FATHER. HE WAS telling a tall tale to Mr. Gibbons, the neighbor. Pennie knew it was a tall tale, but she thought Mr. Gibbons did not. His mouth was open like a caught trout. Pennie knew all about fish. She went fishing with her father every chance he got off work or out of yard work. Taking Pennie fishing was his favorite thing to do. He would tell her tall tales like he was practicing, trying them out on a bit of audience. In the beginning, she just listened. But after years, she began to piece Dad's stories together, and they were slippery tales just like the trout. Once, when she questioned her Dad about the facts in a story, he told her they were fish tales.

"Fish tales are always big, grand," he said.

Pennie decided to try her hand at a fish tale. Her father laughed. She guessed she was good by accident. She had made him laugh, but she had meant her story to be spooky.

Pennie took the threaded hook from her Dad and cast the line. There is a lot of waiting when fishing, and it can be hard to stay focused for a bite. Pennie was trying to come up with another fish tale. Of course, it was about a fish. She was thinking big. She was thinking of a whale that could come and swallow her pole whole. She was pretty tickled by her invention and decided to take it a bit further. She threw her pole into the water to make her whale tale convincing. Her Dad was confused and put out.

"How did you lose your pole?" he said.

She stood in the water. It was cold and lapping up her shins. The slippery moss on the rock where she stood made its way inside her pink Crocs. It was soft and slimy on her feet. She knew to tread lightly lest she fall. Pennie looked at her Dad and unabashedly recited the story about the whale again. Then Pennie waited in eager anticipation for him to applaud her tale. Instead, what happened next left her dumbfounded.

"That is a lie," Dad said. "You do not fib to me. Go sit on the shore and think about what you did. Lying and throwing away a perfectly good rod and reel."

Dad trudged deeper into the water. He was wearing waders. He saw Pennie's fishing pole at the bottom of a clear part of the stream and used his own pole for fishing it out. He returned to the shoreline with entangled poles and a red face. Pennie was unsure what offense she had made. She had done just like he did all the time; she told a fish story. Dad was non-conversant the rest of the afternoon as he untangled poles and cut wire. Finally, the day's trip was over.

The following fishing trip was for Dad and Mr. Gibbons. Pennie was not invited. She sat in the front yard picking dandelions watching her Dad pack up for his trip, which included a cooler full of beer. Dad had always used a much smaller cooler for their trips. Apparently, when you drink beer with a buddy, you must really drink a lot of it, she surmised. She didn't stay to wave goodbye. Pennie rose with a damp bottom from the morning dew and sulked inside. Dad had no eyes for her now. When she entered the house, her nose was assailed with the smell of dog food and last night's dinner. Her mother quietly dusted the living room as Pennie retreated upstairs to her room. She walked over to the oversized fish tank leftover from her Dad's fraternity years. It was a phenomenally large tank for only 6 fish and one little girl. One day Pennie planned to have 20 fish. Twenty seemed like a significant number. She sprinkled in the fish food and watched the fish gather to eat. There were two pearl Gourami, two clownfish (both named Nemo), a bicolor Blenny, and one damselfish (who commanded the tank). Pennie thought they were lovely.

Pennie learned to be quiet that summer. It was easiest. She would not speak back to her father. His chilly demeanor was a silent assault that left her cold. It was far better to bare the lies dripping from his lips than to speak up to the looming figure standing before her, even when she knew better. But more than the silent assault, which rendered her mute. It was the standing-by, not giving voice to the truth, that hacked away at her. Dad's gregarious and pathological lies were wearing on Pennie. When she was around Dad, it was impossible to speak the truth until it became impossible to even talk. So Pennie just kept her mouth shut. At school, they thought she was dumb because she was mute. They placed her in a special classroom. It was loud with the outbursts of the other special children. It was easy for Pennie to hide inside the din. Indeed, her parents must have received a note or invitation to a meeting about her, but they did not show any sign if they had. This she thought was weird, as Dad loved a new audience.

Pennie's silence made her a better listener. She listened to what all her teachers said. Every test was an A.

It was the summer between second and third grade that made a crashing difference. When her father lied to the wrong man, his boss. Dad had bragged about his ability to install a small Koi pond set in elaborate landscaping. In reality, he saw a circular in the junk mail touting the ease of installing a plastic pond basin. Only Pennie's father could convert this cursory glance into a long history of accomplishment. His boss saw a good bargain, and he employed Pennie's father to set to work in his yard on the weekends. Her Dad was already a week overdue on the project and a $1,000 over budget. He had no idea what he was doing. His Google search history was littered with "How to Install a Koi Pond." He learned quickly he did not have all the right tools, but with his supposed history of installing Koi Ponds, this didn't jive. Ever the quick liar, Pennie's father explained to his boss that he had sold off the tools in lean times. The boss increased the budget.

Pennie's dad did what he could to skimp and pocket the money. Pennie's mom kept her mouth shut and packed her husband's cooler with sandwiches and beer. She was nervous. Her husband was lying, telling sloppy stories to his boss of his 9 to 5 job. They couldn't afford to lose that job. Her job at the local library paid very little. Since Pennie never said a peep, it meant she did hear and learn a lot. She understood that Dad's tales were putting the family in danger of losing everything. Pennie didn't have or ask for much, but she did like her bedroom decorated with fish. Even after the fishing debacle last summer, Pennie still loved fish. It was just as well that she stopped fishing because she did want to eat fish. She wanted to be a fish. To swim, free, slicing and swishing through the currents. The light glancing off the water surface above painting rainbows. Pennie wanted to be a mermaid. She didn't think mermaids swam in freshwater, which was just as well to avoid fishermen's hooks. She wanted to swim in the deep with the exotic fish. Pennie wanted to feel and hear the rush of water in her ears, to live in a world without speech.

Her mother was headed out to visit Aunt Bertha, whose sight and smell were failing. Aunt Bertha herself smelled of urine and lavender. She wouldn't even miss Pennie. With her mother's gossamer appearance, Pennie doubted Aunt Bertha would notice her mom's presence. Pennie wondered why her mom was going out of her way to visit Aunt Bertha when her Mom could hardly be put upon to care for Pennie.

So, Pennie was pawned off on her Dad digging a hole in his boss's backyard. It was Pennie's job to make lists of tools needed and to hand over the beers. At first, Pennie's Dad just cussed and grumbled, but after lunch, he started talking. It had been a long time since Pennie had heard him launch into a story. A part of her was eager, and a part of her was disgusted with the sound of his voice. He told a story she'd heard before. He must have forgotten. This time the facts were different. Pennie realized she had no hope of detangling her Dad's accounts from the truth. He was in too deep. He did not know the truth anymore. When Dad's boss came out to check the progress, Pennie's dad took the parts list and added a few expensive items.

"We're going to need these items, Bob," Dad said.

Bob raised an eyebrow and gave Pennie a smile.

"Okay, I gave you my credit card. Do what needs to be done."

In the heat of the day, Dad called it quits.

"No one can work in this heat wave," Dad said. "We'll have to come back tomorrow."

We? Pennie wondered if she was being invited back for a second round. She kind of hoped not. It was hot sitting in the Sun, chasing the shade with her little plastic chair. She could smell the earth baking in the heat, and neither of her parents had thought of sunscreen. On the way home, they stopped at a Home Depot. Pennie walked alongside the cart as her father heaved in everything on the list. Pennie's Dad flirted with the cashier at checkout and said he needed all these materials for his own landscaping company. Pennie thought that very odd as her Dad was a computer programmer. He'd told her he had built Mario Kart. She didn't dare to brag to her friends because she didn't believe him.

Pennie's second day on the job, she wore a St. Louis Cardinals baseball cap. When Dad's boss came out to check on the slow progress, she listened to Dad tell Bob how he had these same setbacks on a pond installation for Ozzie Smith. Bob marveled at how skilled Pennie's Dad was that he was a computer programmer and a landscaper. Pennie's dad said the landscaping was just a side gig he enjoyed when it wasn't 100 degrees outside. Bob told them to take the rest of the day off. Again, they stopped at Home Depot on the way home. Pennie helped Dad load up a cart with the tools they had just purchased yesterday. Next, they made their way to returns. Instead of having the return put back on Bob's card, Pennie's Dad put the cash in his pocket. Pennie looked at the exposed concrete floor as they exited. When they got home, Pennie proceeded to tell on her dad to her mom. His lying was already bad, but stealing was wrong. Dad cut Pennie off and told her to shut her mouth.

"Shush, What you see is not for you to talk about," he said.

"But Dad, stealing is wrong," Pennie said.

"Stealing? I'm not stealing. And I'll not have the likes of you watching me and talking about me. So you keep your damn mouth shut. Do you understand?" he said.

She nodded up and down. She was stymied, but she didn't know if she could obey. The next day Mom ushered her out the door with Dad to return to Bob's house. Pennie hoped her dad would be done taking advantage of his boss soon. When Bob's wife came out with a pitcher of lemonade she tried to make small talk with Pennie.

"What do you want to be when you grow up? A landscaper like your Dad?" she said.

"No," Pennie whispered. "I want to be a mermaid, a professional mermaid," Pennie said.

"Oh, what is a professional mermaid?" the woman said.

"The women in mermaid costumes swimming around in a tank at some bar in Florida or in Disney World."

"Um, oh," the woman said.

"Don't listen to that one. She tells tall tales. She is going to be my partner someday. A fellow landscaper in Pennie's Plants."

Under the lifting laughter of the woman, Pennie felt small and quiet. She didn't know why she ever bothered to speak to adults. It was 6p.m. on a Saturday night in July. Pennie and her dad had to clear out even though there was plenty of sunlight. Bob and his family were having a bar-b-que, and the help, mermaids, and liars too, had to get out. So Dad drove to the Train-wreck Saloon. They sat up at the bar. Dad had another beer, and Pennie had a coke. This place felt too adult to Pennie, so she was sure to keep her mouth shut for as long as she could. But when Dad started hitting on the bartender, Pennie began to get antsy and wriggle about on her stool. When Dad left Pennie sitting there while he went out back with the bartender to have a smoke, which he didn't even smoke, Pennie knew he was lying again.

In the car, Pennie protested about his exodus that left her sitting alone at the bar.

"What were you doing? You don't smoke," Pennie said.

"I was helping her lift some kegs of beer," he said with ease.

"Why? You don't work there," Pennie challenged.

"Shush, keep quiet, and not a word to your mother. Do you hear me?"

"Yes," she whispered.

At dinner, Pennie pushed the food about her plate but ate little. When she climbed the stairs to bed, she didn't even ask for a goodnight kiss, and neither did her parents. Her parents were engrossed in conversation and drinks, having a good time. As she plodded up the stairs, she felt thinner and lighter as if enveloped in silence. When she tried to grouse about her parents' crummy treatment, the words escaped as malformed whispers. She was growing mute. Without words, Pennie no longer had the weight of bearing witness. With no one to hear her, she faded. She stripped off her clothes and gazed at herself in the mirror. She thought she looked a little like a fish, sleek with a pale belly and quiet. She put on her pale green nightgown with smocking across the chest. The gown swam about her, and she felt like a mermaid. Pennie wondered how long a Mermaid could breathe out of water or underwater. The rumble of voices beneath her feet was thankfully unintelligible. She sat on the edge of her bed. She didn't even make a dent. Her head made no shape in her pillow. She was fading. She was consumed in obmutescence. In her mind, she saw her dad's angry face, his puckered lips as he said, "Shush! Shush! Shush!" She didn't feel real anymore. This otherness she was trying on left no room for grief. The grief she left shed on the floor. She crossed the room to her fish tank. She wished she could crawl inside, but she was far too big.

Again, flashing through her mind, "Shush! Shush! Shush!" Pennie felt smaller and refulgent next to the tank as if light from the lamppost outside her window could stream right through her. Pennie was finding it hard to breathe. The rushing sound of her angry dad, "Shush! Shush! Shush!" was beating her down into nothing with no remorse. Pennie was compelled to climb on her dresser, which was quite tricky as she didn't seem to be all there. Now, when she assessed the aquarium, it appeared large and welcoming. She climbed inside. Funny, there was no water displacement. Pennie was a sigh of a girl, a slip of a fish. She was swimming in plain view and yet entirely out of sight. Her silence felt like a natural part of her and not imposed. The water drowned out the sound of her parents, of her dad's lies.

Unchanged Bed Clothes

COLD LIGHT SEEPED INTO THE NIGHT, BREAKING past the wooden slats of closed blinds, spreading like an unwashed virus. It filtered through the empty spaces before becoming lost in the undusted nooks and crannies, an erasable marker of itself. The loud tick of time, knocked out minute by minute, suffocated the passage of the night. The moonlight gave way to the grey morning light, a consistent prize of the widening early morning, pinned to the floor where it cultured a full breath.

Barnes, the dog, provided companionship to this passage of light. Together with the small undecorated Christmas tree that crowded her reading chair, Julie and Barnes determinedly tucked in on the wingback chair. They were sentinels of dawn. Finally, she was tired enough to sleep and crawled between her dirty flannel sheets. With all that was going on, Julie and Kevin still found the passion for staining the sheets. Her satin pillowcase made a slight hiss as she slid her hand along the space awaiting her head. Kevin was sound asleep. He'd kept the sheets warm, and Julie curled up next to him to knock off the chill. She was naked except for her snowman slipper socks. Her feet and her ass were always blocks of ice.

She felt him breathing. How could he sleep and leave her awake, alone? It was this selfish act of abandonment every time he climbed into bed. How could he sleep knowing moment by moment the hospital or police could call? Their son was out, gone for four days in this winter chill. And they could not call the police because he was dealing opioids. They had suspicions that Ben was using drugs until Ben made it clear that using his own product was a bad business move. And he swore his involvement was momentary, just to get enough to pay for college. He was 18, which he had beat into their heads with every conversation. The only method of helping him would be to turn him over to the justice system. And she knew there would be no justice, no help for Ben there. Except he could get his college education in the joint. They started plumbing the depths of morality themselves. What would they be willing to do to avoid student loans? It was a Herculean effort to make coursework affordable. Kevin had suggested divorce, only on paper, to increase their son's odds of financial aid. She thought it was a big gamble, and she was afraid if they opened that door, he might not want to walk back through. Julie knew she was no picnic. She worked until 7 p.m. every night and then came home to work 3 more hours. Never present for a single meal in the house, and the fast-food inner tube was swelling around her middle. It was her tell that she was making poor choices. Julie reached for the Tums on the nightstand and popped a few. Under the twinkling lights of the tree, she chased it with her Xanax. She'd have to call her doctor and get something stronger.

What The Looking Glass Reflects

CAROL LIKED TO STAND IN CORNERS WHEN no one was watching when she was anxious. It calmed her down to tighten her focus on a dried drip of paint, the seam in wallpaper, or a crack in the wall of the visiting Professor's house. Her husband was a professor of History at Sweetgum University.

The booming emptiness of the house, like a quarry, played on Carol's nerves. It reminded her of the children she could not have to fill the large house. Her body was not agreeable to the arrangement of keeping a tenant for more than 3 months. This, too, made her anxious. If she were to dwell on the idea of a baby too long, it required a Xanax and a corner to calm her down.

Staring into the back of William's head while watching a loud Sunday football game was also a trigger. Around 4:30 in the afternoon, each day, that was a trigger. The upside was she had tried many corners in the house and had a rating system based on her sense of urgency. The corner in the small dark dining room with light filtering through the blinds was one of her favorites. She liked this one because she could look askance out the window as if cheating at some game. She also liked the lovely wisteria colored paint that deepened and lightened based on the time of day. The corners became her friends, and she talked to them. Softly, of course, lest Will catch her again.

The first time Will caught Carol standing in a corner was in the bedroom with the blue scrollwork wallpaper. It was outdated just long enough to be trendy with that shabby chic look. She liked to trace the scrollwork with her fingertips. Caught up in a particular favorite curly-que, she did not hear Will coming. Carol stopped her whispering and froze. She could feel Will staring at her back. With a great effort that made her eyes sting, she turned to him and said, "It is just the most lovely design." Will agreed and ushered her from the room. The next morning the corner was filled with a large, gilded full-length mirror made from Sweetgum. She must have spent one too many times in the corner. She wondered how Will got it into the room while she slept, her head hammered from that one glass of wine. The mirror was enormous, with a gilt wood frame from floor to ceiling. It was carved with five-point star leaves. Her anger with Will for filling her corner was ebbing.

Perhaps a mirror makes a better coping mechanism. This mirror may be just the therapy Carol needed. Sure, it was just another crutch, but you need a crutch sometimes. She climbed out of bed and followed the details of the carvings. She smiled, a little smile though it was, at herself with the glow of her face in the flattering daylight. With the heat of the day on her face, Carol climbed back into bed and soon napped. She woke from lilting little giggles. Of course, no one was there, but a single gold stud earring and her wooden knitting needles were resting on the bedclothes. It was as if someone had gone about snatching her things just to return them as gifts.

As late afternoon set in, Carol sat in bed with a book and a pint of *Ben and Jerry's Chunky Monkey* ice cream. She must have dozed off because she woke with her hand in a puddle of melted ice cream and the pint on the floor. It was growing dark. Moonlight was on the heels of the fading day. It filtered through the window, creating little dancing lights upon the looking glass. It was almost as if there was movement inside. Quietly, she tiptoed to the mirror. It was swimming like water, and a small chubby face and arm reached out of the glass, beckoning Carol to enter. Carol froze in awe at the visage of a cherub, a baby in the looking-glass, inviting her into an orchard of Sweetgums. Abruptly, she heard Will enter with the dull thud of the front door. When Carol turned back to the mirror, it was solid. "NO," she cried and slammed the palm of her hand against the mirror. There was a heart-breaking crack that ran through the mirror and disappeared in ripples of reflection. With bloody palms and bare feet, Carol entered the looking glass. Will ran up the stairs to his wife's cry of "NO." The room was empty. No one was home.

If I Could Cry, I'd Be Happier

I AM WOMAN. FOR CENTURIES UPON CENTURIES, tears and sex have been my tools, my defense, my weapons. But you browbeat, belittled, and berated me until the tears dried up. And with the exodus of tears, my libido shortly followed. I feel like crying, but I can't. Your cold cruelty shut me down. I buckle, bend, and cringe, but my eyes are dry. Without tears, the world thinks I'm strong, but they couldn't be more wrong. I am robbed of the release, the declaration of my pain. I am a husk of a woman. I'd punish you by withholding sex, a time-honored tradition, but that well has dried up. I cannot withhold what we don't have. I have no outlets for my pain and my passion, except food. I've grown considerably large, but my size doesn't concern you. You are only offended. I had thought it impossible that you could view me as more of an albatross around your neck, but my form has proven otherwise. You engage with other women. I am not jealous about the sex and affection. Instead, I wonder if you allow their tears. Do you break them as you've broken me? Don't mistake me; you didn't break my heart. You never had my heart. Someone beat you to that, but he left me with my tears, at least. You instead methodically pulled at the threads that held me together, lifting each stitch like a spiteful seamstress. Before I knew what was happening, I was unraveling, falling apart. I tried to sew me back together, but it was sloppy and scarred. I look like a poorly cared for ragdoll, easy to abuse.

I am discarded. I wait in the shadows for your punch. Every day another undoing, and I have no hope for something else. I have nowhere to go. I only know that if I could cry, I'd be happier. Upon your return, you lectured. You raised your voice just a bit, not enough to make me flinch, just enough to make me listen. Your sardonic laugh broke the threshold. I sat on the floor with the dog, brewing toward the apex of my anger to spew forth my bottled comments sitting at a simmer, but I tamp them down. Without my tears, I am too dry and brittle to make a countermove. I notice the dust bunnies under the coffee table, so fragile and undesirable, so dry, a collection of nothing, just like me.

Another day in the shadows, in the corners, I notice something has been sown. It has germinated deep within me, a sorrow over my dwindling demise. It wells up. It remembers me before your heavy foot. A victory tear beads up in the corner of my eye, a trickle unleashed in a steady stream. I feel clean again, and you will not defeat me. Your words have molted. They've become flimsy, backed only with your own insecurities and lies. My tears are a hot dripping restoration of me, an inner beauty of absolution. I will not stay and share my tears with you. They are my own. I pack my things in that worn-out duffle graying under the bed. I pack my things and weep. I hiccup with deep liberating sobs. My step is lighter as I leave; my tears belong to me. My words have returned. You caused me pain. You took from me an essential element of being, but I took it back. You have no power over me. My face is wet and glorious.

The Days of Bacon

STARTING IN HER 20S AND INTO HER MARRIED years, Miriam was a vegetarian. It wasn't always so. Rewind the clock, and find her wobbling in the unsteady gait of a two-year-old down the little garden path between the houses. She's sniffing the neighbor's lush bloom of Peonies with the whole thrust of her chubby face; meanwhile, her Bubbe walks behind her, carrying a small plate of her very best china topped with tender, crispy bacon for the princess in Pampers. Grandparents are notorious for spoiling their grandchildren, but no one had any idea it would go this far.

Then came the gluttonous adolescence. Miriam demanded bacon at every meal. Bubbe could smell the forbidden scent of bacon on her hands and in Miriam's hair. It was impossible to clean that bacon grease away in time for shul.

Finally, Miriam said goodbye to bacon when she met Abe. The stress, the smell eventually faded for Bubbe and Miriam. Years and children, bar mitzvahs, and bat mitzvahs roll by until Abe passed early in his 50s. At the funeral, Bubbe thought she detected a whiff of bacon and said a prayer.

Miriam, like anyone, did not know how to grieve. She had the support and comfort of mourning from her and Abe's congregation. She tore her clothing and covered the mirrors, but she lacked the depth of surrender required to let Abe go. Miriam needed to fill the gap left in her life. She was still sitting Shiva, but her body yearned for the consolation of a man. Miriam set boundaries to Shiva and stepped outside the community to Abe's long-time gentile friend, Andy.

At four in the morning, Miriam woke to the smell of bacon. It hailed back to her youth, and it diminished Miriam's grief just enough.

"Are you making breakfast?" she called as she rose from the bed.

"Don't come in here. I'm making you breakfast in bed."

Miriam slid back between the sheets. She pulled the flat paisley sheet up and tucked it tightly around her breasts to give them a little support, coverage, or something. The thick smell of sizzling bacon filled the room. Andy returned with a plate piled high with bacon and two Bloody Marys balanced on a tray. The grease was on their lips and fingers, slowly covering every inch of skin with salt and fat. Miriam was a mess, and she loved it.

On the Rim of Your Whims

I T WAS AN IRISH FUNERAL. WE WERE IRISH IN THE sense that I was the 5th generation removed from Ellis Island. I had always doubted that Great, Great Grandpa coming into America through the trials and tedium of Ellis Island, but when I was 14 I won a Boy Scout contest for my short story about immigration. I made the whole thing up, but I did win a trip to the big apple for the entire family for two days. We spent a good chunk of that time looking up Great, Great Grandpa in the book. We never found him. Dad shook the whole thing off and took us up to the Statue of Liberty. Maybe we weren't so very Irish, my siblings and I thought. But Dad clung to the ancestry of Callahan, like a babe with a security blanket. I think he was unable to share the doubt nettled deep into his identity. St. Patrick's day continued to smell of corn beef and cabbage, and Dad and Mom continued to get sloppy drunk. Me and my sister, Irene, were the eldest of our brood of 5. She and I washed the dishes, setting them into the broken dishwasher to dry.

Dad was proud of my immigration story.

"It's a good lie, but don't let that go to your head. You know what, you should come down to the pub with me and read it to the boys."

I rode my bike down during sunset. Dad was already three sheets to the wind, so he didn't notice me for a good 20 minutes. He faced the herculean feat of setting me up on the bar to the bartender's protest when he did. He stumbled a bit in my resurrection. I landed on my right knee and had to raise myself in qualmish embarrassment to my feet. I stepped in someone's lamb stew, and it soaked through my sock to the ankle. I didn't want to be there. I was a loser, by all counts from my father.

"Boy, did you paint that fence like that?"

"You're some kind of slacker getting a D in geometry."

"Where's your sense of humor when I insult you?"

"Come here, try a shot of whiskey. Well, don't cough like a girl about it."

Now, I was expected to muster Irish courage. Only I was supposed to do it without Dad and his chums' liquid courage. I needn't have worried about my performance. No one paid me any mind after the first paragraph as long as the lilt of my voice went on. To test my theory, I embarked on the Humpty Dumpty nursery rhyme to thunderous applause. I was tired and wanted to go home, but Dad insisted on closing the place down. When I finally saw my exit, the bartender and a couple of patrons insisted that Dad not drive home. I found myself on the wrong end of a swap. Dad was perched on my bike, riding away from me in herky-jerky movements. I had the keys to the car. I drove standing. It was the only way I could reach the petals. We made it home alive.

"Not a word to your mother. Do you understand that?"

He laughed in my ear. It was a rough, wet whisper of a laugh. It was just the beginning of a long set of lies I was to keep from my mother. Do you know what a history of lies does to a relationship? It bars any intimacy or friendship from developing. She didn't fully understand why, but she knew she could not trust me. You'd think I developed an estranged relationship with my parents. But I did not; I stay parked at 4252 Telegraph Road. I moved into the basement. My siblings moved out. I had my wings clipped by Dad and his needy stretch into my life. Everything I did was detailed with our Irish sins.

I was drunk when I entered the funeral parlor. I could see his profile in the casket. I hugged my way to the front, and I tucked an open bottle of whiskey inside with Dad. I hadn't written a speech. What would it say?

"Dad, you were an alcoholic, not Irish. You stood in my way to life. All I ever wanted was to be important to you, but the only person that could ever shine in your eyes was yourself, all covered in your own bullshit." No one asked me to say anything. No one trusted me. No one deemed my memories important enough. When we backed out of the room. I was not a pallbearer. I was not steady enough on my feet. Shit, I carried him all my life, and now in death, I'm still not good enough for any of them. While Dad was buried in the lies and glories that come in part with a funeral, it was I who could give a bare-bones eulogy. Exactly why I wasn't chosen for an honored role of his interment. In the corner was a lone man familiar from the pub, and he played Danny Boy on the fiddle. It was my name, but he wasn't playing for me. He was just another whim of my Dad.

The Rome Club

THERE WERE SIX OF THEM, EACH THERE for the same reason: Big Mike, Vince, Joe, Tommy, Sal, and Frank. The Rome Club was an old country tradition. They had buried a bottle of wine in a secret location. The last two men living were to dig it up and drink a toast to the others. They sat at a round oak table at the back of Milo's restaurant right next to the exit leading to the Bocce Ball courts in the yard. Every Sunday, they would play bocce ball; then bust each other's balls over wine the rest of the afternoon before heading home to their wives (those who still had wives) for supper.

Frank was the most vocal, and that was saying something in this crowd. Six old Italians in it for the game of their life. Without telling their wives, they each pitched a grand into the pot. The last man standing wins. No foul play. Just natural causes. The first one out was Joe, which was to be expected as he had a good ten years on the rest of them. They all attended the funeral, and they continued the club with Joe's chair tilted towards the table. Years later, Vince had a heart attack, and Big Mike followed him 3 weeks after. Two more chairs tipped into the table. No more bocce ball, just coffee, and arguments. Even Tommy, Sal, and Frank felt the table fall quiet between bickering. Everything was a row from politics to who tipped better. But they never fought about who would be the last man standing. They use to, and now it felt like a jinx. Big Mike had bragged he'd outlive them all two days before the big one.

Sundays at Milo's were slow and dark, with sunlight filtering through the Italian flags hung in the windows. The old guys were regulars, a part of the atmosphere. It felt like a place out of time until they looked at the tilted chairs, beating like a heart out of step. Tommy went quietly in his sleep, unexpectedly. Frank and Sal took it hard. With a choked-up Saluda, they drank to Tommy from the unearthed wine and tilted his chair. Then they never said another word.

Frank and Sal hated each other. They lived on the Hill, a small section of St. Louis inhabited by the descendants of Italian and Sicilian immigrants. It was impossible not to have friends in common. But they had always argued the loudest, the hottest. They never could mend the past. Frank married Delores, and Sal would never forgive him. He still held a special place for Delores. She'd been the prettiest girl on the Hill, and she wasn't even from the Hill. She was a nice Irish girl who was friends with Josephine from St. Teresa's All Girl's School, just 4 blocks over from Milo's, in fact. The first time Sal saw her, he knew she was the only one for him. Her auburn hair and blue eyes were beautiful, and that smile shone with all the hope and promise a G.I. needed going off to war. As Fate would have it, while Sal stormed the beach at Normandy, Frank, too young yet to go to war, would steal his girl. Frank wound up on the clean-up crew in Japan, sending home exotic trinkets to Delores, his fiancé. Sal was lucky to be stuck in an army hospital for months.

All these years, the two men lived in jealousy and hatred. The insults and slights, the public snubbing and shaming for decades. Now, it was just the two of them at the table with four tilted chairs. Sal walked into Milo's and waved at the bartender as he lumbered to the back table with his newspaper tucked under his arm. He liked to read every page of the paper, but if you had asked him, he'd said the paper was there to keep him from having to look at Frank's ugly mug. When Sal got to the obituaries, there was Frank Cunetto listed. He tipped the chair and started to smile. He'd won. He sat there alone, and he began to cry.

Incarceration Nation

The Yard

"Hey, Skippy," Mac said. "I never thought I'd find you here."

Skippy knew the voice; he turned around to face Scott Mackenzie.

He wasn't prepared to see Mac here at the prison, at least not as a Defense Officer. This guy was a fuckin' prick. He extended his hand in an approximation of peace, anyway. Skippy felt the cement block walls scraping, grinding, closing in on him. Already, the confines of the prison were pushing the parameters of his mild case of claustrophobia. Mac hesitated, then gave him a firm handshake and leaned in for a pat on the back.

"Skippy and I go way back to elementary school. We took Wood Shop together in high school," Mac said to the gathering of guards.

"No one calls me Skippy anymore," he said. "It's Mort."

"Mortimer is more like it," Mac said with a grin. "But Skippy is classic, Man. Are you sure you want to drop it?"

"Yes."

"Well, that hurts a little. I remember calling you Skippy cause you used to skip down the halls past all the girls and the fairies. Hey, you didn't come here lookin' for fairies, did you?"

"No, I'm married," Mort said.

Mort's tone was a gentle freeze, which the other DOs were feeling out, but the coldness in his voice went straight over Mac's head.

Mac took the lead on the brigade of DOs in the level six housing, which contained the low-level felons of Sweetgum County. Most of these men were serving 364 days max. It made for a quick rollover, but many of these guys were also repeat offenders. It wasn't their first time in this unit. It made for hot heads rooking the frightened and defensive newbies. Mostly, these inmates were more puff than punch. Mac was always looking for trouble, though. He picked fights with the weaker links; the other DOs looked the other way. Mort cut a slice off the past and steeled his demeanor against Mac's harsh rock face. He wouldn't make waves.

"Alright, saddle up to your positions. Skippy, you're with me. I'll show you the rounds," Mac said. "Now, the thing you need to know around here is the inmates divide themselves into race gangs. We're supposed to close that shit up. But you'd need more guards than we got to fight that battle. So, we just jump in and bust some skulls when they get out of hand. 'Ya know?"

"Yeah, I get it. We don't care about prejudice, but we don't want a race war."

"Well, if you get a race war on your hands. You want to make sure the Whites win," he said.

Mac and Mort walked the pods, checked random cells, and generally let the prisoners know who was in charge.

"Now, this prison can get pretty boring. The prisoners aren't that tough. But a good way to get them riled up is to do a shakedown. Take some contraband from storage and plant it during a "random" cell check. Then take them to the hole. It's hilarious. They know what you did, but they don't dare say a word. It's pretty good fun. But don't overdo it. It'll put a load of hurt on you from the warden," Mac said.

Mort was feeling underprepared. Before this gig, he'd been a mall cop, which was a position that held no power or respect, just a lot of hotfoot pursuit of kids he didn't want to bust anyway. It was a cake job with no consideration. When the mall was failing, there was an uptick in shoplifting from the kids and employees. No one cared, not Mort. He wouldn't send any of these kids off to actual cops when the whole thing was coming down around them anyway. At Gateway Malls, his security position lingered to let real estate agents show the space to potential buyers, but nobody was buying. Gateway Mall owners made a getaway to someplace without jurisdiction, and the mall was fated to demolition. After the "Skippy" nickname reveal in the first hour on the new job, Mort decided to keep his job history as a mall cop a secret from all.

"How was the first day?" Ashley said. "I made your favorites, oatmeal, everything cookies. I have a plate straight from the oven."

Mort decided to keep the snags in his day to himself. He didn't want Ashley to worry about him or his job security. Mort reflected briefly on how his wife was supposed to be the one person he could say anything to, but in this case, she was the key person he couldn't say anything to. He thought this is how affairs start when one of you starts looking for someone else to confide in, and the adultery becomes shared confidence between you and another. Thus, stripping the marriage of all the supports that keep it together. Mort knew because he had seen it happen to his sister Angela. Mort made a mental note to tell Ashley about his day, someday later, and this is how he kept his marriage in its self-inflicted confines of pleasantries.

It was three months in on the job, and the other guards did him a solid and kept the Skippy shit to themselves. Mort would have breathed a sigh of relief, but no one does that in prison.

Inmate Hill had a juice card. He was one of the long-term inmates, and he had an in with DO Mac. The two had been working together for two years now. Mac smuggled the cocaine in on his person by packing the rabbit and then shitting it out once he was inside the prison. Hill distributed it inside the 6th floor. It was easier to get the drugs in than to get the money out. The money was bulkier and had to be stashed in payouts with Hill. Mac knew Hill was sampling the product, but he didn't fancy any other inmate to trust with the arrangement. Then there was a new installation on the

6th floor. A large, fit man in for drug contraband. He was a dark man with a bald head and an angry goatee framing his mouth like a lookout to his gold teeth. This man rarely spoke, but when he did, he put his subject in their place. He was flavored with all the slang, which told of prior arrests. He was also educated, marking him as a college man or at least a community college man. This new inmate, Farrow, took the lead position of the Blacks two days after arrival, and it only took standing on the neck of his predecessor, Hill, to do so.

It was Farrow that approached Mac. He let Mac feel in control as he kept his head bowed during the discussion as if the negotiations were something Mac wanted. Mac left the 6th floor for his lunch break, feeling smug. This was just what he'd been looking for a man who didn't use the product, and Farrow agreed to only take 20% off the top. Farrow's smooth speech made Mac feel smart, which was something Mac never felt.

"So, we're in the car?" Farrow asked.

"Yeah, but if things get hot in here. I expect you to nip it in the butt," Mac said.

"Nip it in the bud," Farrow said.

"What? That's what I said, nip it in the butt."

The inmates laughed in their sleeves, even if they didn't get the malapropism. They would take any opportunity to laugh at a guard.

The next day Mac and Mort made a random bunk check, and this is when Mac's sleight of hand placed the Coke under Farrow's mattress. Farrow gave Mac the slightest bow of his head while he looked Mort dead in the eye. Farrow had ambitions beyond the 6th floor and Mac. He got on the bowl with toilet talk. Farrow had taken the plastic spoons he'd smuggled out of the lunchroom. He took out his stash of Styrofoam cups and carved the bottoms out with a sharpened spoon handle. He made a thin rope out of somebody else's torn-up sheet, and he tied it to the interspersed spoons. It was time to go fishing. He flushed the toilet, and his roomie, Jamison, scooped out the returning water. This left him with an empty bowl. He placed his tower of cups in the bowl and attempted to contact someone on the fifth floor. It was a muffled success. Someone named Pinky, on the fifth floor, struck an agreement with Farrow. Little baggies of cocaine were trafficked this way through the talking toilets. Making contact and doing business was even smoother with the ladies on the seventh floor. It took a little longer to complete the transaction due to the flirting, but it was worth it. Janice became Farrow's right hand on the seventh floor. It didn't matter that he couldn't see her or that she was white. Her voice was enough to satisfy Farrow. He was sure to repeal toilet privileges from his roomie for Janice's sake. Jamison, the roomie, was forced to use another cell's toilet to keep the boo-boo out of the talking toilet. Janice got pissy when shit arrived along with her coke.

Mac intimidated the guards to look the other way, which only bred more corruption. The prison tower was a rickety form of collusion, which was only being held together with the general feeling of hopelessness and the taste of cocaine. When a new guard hit the ground with something to prove, Mac was not about to bring attention to himself. The new guard, Brady, was fast to ferret out the cocaine distribution revealed in a toilet transaction scam. Brady was able to take down Janice, but Farrow eluded him. In the sudden halt of drug trafficking, Farrow took over Pruno production, jail alcohol made from fruit, bread, and sugar. It wasn't as lucrative as cocaine, but it was less risk and more payment since he'd cut Mac out of the equation. But there were limitations. Pruno was a weak replacement, and it could only be distributed on the same floor it was brewed. Mort kept his mouth shut. Mac was furious.

To blow off steam after work, Mort turned to his hobby of making lamps at home. He made lamps out of used champagne bottles. He filled them with marbles so they wouldn't be top-heavy, then he added the electrical housing, a bulb, and a shade. The lamps made a clean $55 profit on Etsy. It was a nice supplement to his income. Ashley had her own Etsy account making steampunk costumes for a more extensive customer base than most people would think. This current lamp Mort was working on was an order from another guard, Ray. He wasn't a bad sort like some of the guards that bullied and barked at the men serving time. Of course, the guards had to demand respect and carry the upper hand somehow, but Mort thought he could do it without being a racist, drug-pushing dick.

Mort observed the complex issuance of racism that came from Mac. Mac was overtly interested in the black gang and Farrow. He took opportunities that weren't even there to beat down and throw the black men in the hole, except Farrow, of course. Farrow was a wild card, which just needled Mac. Mac could feel his position as alpha male slipping between his fingers. More jaunts and jabs were directed toward Mort during this upheaval of power. It made Mort uncomfortable, but he understood to face-off with another guard inside the jail would be career suicide. And if he didn't win that beat down, he was practically asking for a shank, three knees deep.

It was a Thursday morning out in the yard. There was a fine mist hung in the humidity from the rain the night before. Mort could feel the tension from the cutoff of cocaine and the compression of stress, biding its time. Mac was prowling the perimeter of the yard, his body language threatening to pounce without prevarication. Violence often rang out in a blind spot on the security cameras. Just out of sight, a fight broke out in the yard using the wall of men's bodies as full coverage. The inmates egged the fighters on. A skinny, lower-ranked white man was vying to raise his position amongst his own by picking a fight with Farrow. The white man was just selling wolf tickets with his empty threats. Suddenly, the sound of a naked slap of skin on skin, encouraged by a sea of onlookers, took Mort back.

IT WAS HOT. The kind of hot that even the children wondered why the teachers had allowed them to go outside. Sarah Franklin sat on a swing in the full Sun. If she had moved, she'd at least have a breeze, Mort thought. Mort wiggled to make his body smaller, to keep him in the small patch of shade provided by sitting under the slide. He could hear the kids clustered overhead under the dome of the slide. Someone came down the burning metal slide with a swoosh and landed with a crush on the small pebbled grounds. The smell of seared flesh was in the air. It was Mac; he approached Sarah and demanded she get off the swing. Sarah, never too bright, just stared at him under the beating Sun. Mac pushed her, and she tumbled off the swing backward under the sneering laughter of Mac. Mort had never been one to stand up to Mac, and he didn't see any reason to start now. A gnawing grew in his stomach as he watched Sarah cry big, silent tears. His tears went down his throat hard like a rock.

MAC WATCHED THE FIGHT from his station against the fence, a good 500 feet away from the action, and then he crossed the yard and stepped up to the edge of the fray. With the addition of Mort's approach, the prisoners slowed their roll. They parted and pieced out across the yard. Mac grabbed Farrow by the hair and pushed his face into the ground with more force than necessary.

He cuffed Farrow and slipped something into the back of his pants. As he helped Farrow to his feet, the white fighter reached in with a blow to Farrow's ribs. Mac laughed and released Farrow. Mort pushed and peeled his way into the loosened ring of men. Shaking off the memory of Mac on the playground. Mort demanded the white prisoner stand down. The prisoner wiped a streak of blood from his mouth and put his hands in the air with confidence that his ass was protected by his skin color. Mort cuffed the white man with bloody knuckles and a smirk. Then he looked up from his prisoner to see Mac subtly shaking his head no.

"They were both fighting," Mort said.

Mac gave a curt nod, yes. The four crossed the shortest distance across the yard to the metal staircase inside the doors.

"Farrow, I'm going to hold on to your cuffs so you don't fall going down the stairs," Mac said.

After three steps down, Mac let go of Farrow and kicked him in the back. Farrow made a steep plunge down the metal stairs with a sickening smack against the painted concrete floor, but no one came. Blood and teeth were on the floor. Farrow had been knocked out. Mort and his prisoner scuttled quickly down the stairs. The inmates in the yard pressed against the window in the door, pushing and shoving for a look. Mort walked away from his charge. He stepped up to Mac, who was standing there smiling.

"No one laughs at me," Mac said.

Mort throat punched Mac, and Mac dropped to his knees, making coughing and gagging noises. The cheering from outside was in concert. The yard rallied as one against the man. Mort's prisoner shuffled back and bowed his head. Mort worried about his job, but it was needless. After that event, Mac was transferred to another housing with harder men who wouldn't be bullied by his lily-white ass. Mort decided his fate. Two weeks later, Mort delivered a lamp to the new DO Ray and made his departure from the prison. He didn't do it, but he felt like he could skip.

Lip Blam

L IPS ARE GROSS IF YOU WATCH THEM IN MOTION
wet, dry, rough, soft, flaky, luscious, spittle, and
bad breath. So Harlow asked for her tube of lip
balm from Orderly Roberts.

"Can I have my lip blam?" Harlow asked. "You see,
my lips are so chapped," she said with a pout.

"Okay, give me a minute. I have to give out meds,"
Orderly Roberts said.

"Here you go," he said and handed over the little
tube of Orange Crush chapstick. Roberts didn't think
her lips looked chapped. He figured it was just something to do when stuck on the ward and watched as
she applied it to her pale lips. He fantasized about
what those lips would look like with a bold, red color
like his sister wore. Roberts was just an orderly, but
he felt some of the patients were misplaced and mis-
managed. In his mind, Harlow was one of them. If it
weren't for the morning and evening rounds of meds,
Roberts would have no indication of Harlow's condition. She was Bi-Polar and went off her meds from
time to time, and every time she landed in the hospital. But she straightened out pretty much by the time
she reached the main population ward where Roberts

worked. He was jerked out of his reverie by an outburst from Oliver. This guy had been in much longer than insurance customarily allowed. He had nowhere else to go. No family, no place to stay, the social workers had promised him he would be released three days ago, and this quiet guy who shuffled the floors like an old man, which belied his 23 years, was frustrated. The Nurses' station housed Cafe and De-Cafe urns of coffee along with Styrofoam cups and little packets of sugar. The objects were now being hurled at the nurses. Roberts embraced Oliver in a stifling hug and worked him to the floor. Another Orderly joined the struggle armed with a syringe of Midazolam. Together, Roberts and Orderly Harrison muscled Oliver back to his room to sleep his anger off. When Roberts regained the floor, the other inmates were whispering and wide-eyed. Harlow approached him and released the chapstick in Robert's hand.

"Here's the lip blam," she said.

"You know it's balm, right?"

"What?" she said, shrinking from Roberts.

"It's lip balm, not blam," Roberts said gently.

"Oh, right. I get confused," Harlow said.

Roberts felt wrong for correcting her. He didn't want to scare Harlow off. He only had her for three more days, and then she was getting out. He couldn't ask for her phone number. It was an impossible relationship. Roberts palmed the lip balm back in her hand.

"Keep it. Just be discrete," he said.

He gave himself the same advice.

Roberts wasn't working when Harlow was released. He resigned himself to the inevitable. His purpose was to help those short-term cases get back on the right path. It started out as rewarding, but some of these people just seemed to be arrested on the fringe of society, not a danger to it. But, of course, he was no doctor. He was the muscle.

Time inside an asylum sucks the staff and the patients into a warped fabric of reality, and the days run a cycle of drama and drool. Roberts began to wonder who was really incarcerated in this place, him or the patients? Charlotte slinked up the hall and cornered him up against the wall, mumbling, " Do you identify as a hero? Do you identify as a hero? Do you identify..."

Charlotte's repetition of this question was maddening, and it got inside Roberts' head like an earworm. He would ask himself the question on break and off shift. Was he a hero or a medical thug? His time in the asylum was tortured and terminal. Who was really trapped in this place?

A new patient, James, was obsessed with his missing shoes, and tension was high in his demeanor. He shouted out threats to the unknown persons that had his shoes.

"Where's my kicks?" James pleaded.

"You can't have your shoes here. You got the gripper socks," Roberts said.

"Man, I don't want no gripper socks. I want my kicks. Then I'll kick your ass," James shouted.

"I need you to keep it down and stop the threats," Roberts said.

"You telling me what to do? I don't think so, Bitch," James said and pushed Roberts back.

Roberts got him in a prone floor hold. Orderly Harrison fastened the restraints. Then, hopped up on adrenaline, the Orderlies lifted the man and strapped him to the table in the solitary room. The rest of the inmates made a reticent scatter to their rooms.

It was the end of the summer, Roberts had a much-needed three-day weekend. He and his buddies, Marc and Lucas, were meeting up at Milo's for some beers and bocce ball. And to be honest, they were hoping to hook up with some babes. Marc fetched the first round of beers while Lucas and Roberts wrestled up the bocce balls and chalk to mark the score. Then, Marc returned with a trio of girls, and introductions were made.

"So, what do you do?" the strawberry blonde Twiggy asked Roberts.

"Oh, stay away from him. He'll lock you up," Marc said.

"What are you some kind of cop?"

"Naw, he's an orderly over at the mental hospital. Spends all day with the loonies," Marc said.

After the last pitch of the bocce ball, the ladies begged off and went in pursuit of less creepy conversation.

The guys were still quarreling over who was responsible for scaring the ladies off when they entered a greasy spoon, the Midnight Owl.

Roberts did not like owls. He got a plush owl on his 8th birthday. Since then, every birthday and Christmas, he was gifted another owl. Things had really gotten out of hand when his grandma got him a set of owl salt and pepper shakers when he was 14. This diner's name had kept him away, but tonight the dining victory went to Marc and Lucas. Roberts kept his head down in the menu, avoiding the Owl clocks, toys, and taxidermy on the walls. The waitress smelling of bacon was rattling off specials. She started to recite the Midnight Owl special when Roberts looked up into her face. No introduction was needed. It was a greasy Harlow with her hair up and thick eyeliner. It was Harlow right in front of him. But she didn't let on that she knew him. Roberts assumed, correctly, that Harlow didn't want to be identified. But this understood anonymity did not stop her from zoning in on Roberts and flirting aggressively.

Roberts excused himself for the bathroom. In the narrow back hall, Harlow stood in his way, "It's so nice to see you," she said.

Roberts was unsettled. What were the odds of them meeting like this? He ate up her attention, and his fantasies about her came crowding back in his head and cluttered his judgment.

"Let's go somewhere more private," she said.

"Ah, yes," he said with bated breath.

After a greasy meal of eggs, onions, and hash, the guys made their goodbyes. Roberts settled into his black 1967 Chevy Impala and waited. Roberts was racking his brain for a private place. There was a Red Roof Inn four miles down the road, but they never made it there. Harlow unbuckled her seatbelt and leaned dangerously close to Roberts' face, for starters.

"Hey, hey, you need to put your seatbelt back on," he said.

But she was busy fishing for something in her purse. It was a tube of Orange Crush chapstick.

"Here's some lip blam for you," she said, smearing it across his open mouth and chin.

A clump stuck on his bottom teeth. Roberts wiped and at it with the cuff of his sleeve while Harlow redoubled her attack and swung her right leg over Roberts. Then, saddling him, Harlow began to grind.

"Harlow, I can't see. Get off," he said.

"I thought you liked me?" she said. "You're no fun."

Harlow was pouting and leaning against her door with angst that scared Roberts. Just then, he saw the lights in his rearview mirror, and it was backed by the siren. Roberts pulled over on the shoulder of the road. This was a busy road during the day, but the businesses were all shut down at night, and the four-lane road was a vast playground for drunk drivers on the way home.

"What's going on here?" Officer Manners asked.

His flashlight illuminated the half-dressed Harlow slumped along the window.

"Do you want to have a good time, Officer," Harlow said, climbing back over Roberts. Roberts was glad to have the policeman's assistance. Harlow was out of control.

"Step out of the car," Officer Manners said to Roberts.

"Me? What about her?"

With that, Harlow stepped from the car and planted a handstand on the side of the road. Her waitress uniform fell down around her waist. She was naked, waist down. Roberts looked to see her panties draped from his rearview mirror. He had no idea when that happened.

Officer Manners made Roberts take a breathalyzer test, which he failed, and found himself cuffed in the backseat of the squad car. A second squad car arrived to take the loud and hard-to-handle Harlow to the psych ward. She'd been wearing her medical ID bracelet.

Robert's car had been impounded, and he was unable to release it until Tuesday. He drove straight from the impound yard to work. He told his supervisor that he would need time off for his court date. Roberts thought this was the height of his embarrassment, but he was wrong.

"Hey, there lip blam, man," Harlow said in a scratchy voice.

She moved in close, not too close, just close enough so only he could hear her when she dropped her voice.

"How much trouble did you get into?"

"Plenty. But you need to stay away from me." Roberts said.

"Awww. Don't you like me when I'm manic? But, admit it, I'm much more fun."

"No, I don't. We can't act like that in here."

"You mean you can't act like that in here. I can do whatever I want. I rather thought I got that point across this weekend," Harlow said. "It's not about you."

Roberts stared into those big brown eyes. But he stopped seeing what he wanted to see. He saw a woman that needed help, stability. And what had he done but take her for a joy ride? He felt like a misogynistic ass. Harlow slipped off like a discarded garment and curled up in a green faux leather chair. Roberts watched her sitting there, talking to herself. A patient approached Roberts from the left. It was Charlotte. She was to be transferred to a long-term facility that day. Charlotte stopped to rub the top of Harlow's tussled hair.

"Do you identify as a hero?" she asked Roberts. "Do you?"

Library Dues and Don'ts

SHE HAD TO LAY ON HER STOMACH TO SWEEP her arm under the kids' beds, brushing her fingertips on the items just out of reach: a baseball glove, a math textbook, and Mr. Grumbles the blue elephant. Her long brown hair was entangled with dust bunnies that she shook free from her shoulders when she sat up. Vicki was determined to return all of the stray library books that were spread out on the shelves, tossed in corners, and buried under the kids' toys in the toy bin and clothes in the closet. It took her several trips to load up the car, but she returned all the children's overdue library books. She made the first installment payment on the fines of $30 per week for the next month.

Vicki filled the children's stomachs with glasses of water to keep the hunger pangs at bay so they might fall asleep without suffering. After she tucked the children in bed, she started drinking his Busch beer. Vicki was nervous he would find out about the library fees, and he would beat her. She was anxious he would taste the beer on her breath, and he would beat her, but he came home in an affable mood. Damon, too, had been drinking and something more. He pulled a small wrinkled baggy out of his King's jacket pocket and dumped it on the table with a few loose coins and his wallet. Damon stumbled off to the bathroom. Vicki walked away from a hot stove with the last of the hamburger helper and the meat. A meager meal that wouldn't stave off hunger. A waste they'd never eat. She padded over to the baggie of snow and fingered the fine powder. She rubbed a small amount on her gums. She didn't have to wait long. Vicki retired to the living room, absorbed in the show she was bingeing, Supernatural. Damon was suddenly by her side. Without provocation, he slapped her across the face. Then punched her straight on, breaking her nose again. He'd done this before when high on cocaine and when stone-cold sober. She felt the blood dribble down from her nose and over her split lip. She quickly climbed from the floor, grabbed the oversized, filthy ashtray with a stray piece of gum from one of the kids, and she cracked him upside the head. He was so numb from the cocaine he didn't even feel it, but he staggered backward into a kitchen chair, shattering the hand-me-down wooden chair in pieces. He stabilized himself and lunged at her with a grunt and a thud at her feet. The weight he capitulated knocked her down. Vicki ran her fingers across the floor like a spider looking for anything to protect herself. Damon lurched over her. He was bleeding. In his face, there was a grotesque distortion. He looked like a vampire in his snarl and dripping blood. Vicki plunged the weapon in hand into his chest. She aimed for his heart. But she punctured a lung with a kitchen knife, not his heart with a wooden stake.

They lay in a heap, which is how the children found them under a thick billow of smoke from the kitchen, which smelled like burnt meat and hamburger helper. They wondered why they hadn't been offered any food. The children, Maxwell, 11, and Ellen, 8, called 911. The domestic abuse was over for this household. The Tuffins were dismantled.

After three months in the court system, a relieved Vicki Tuffin was sentenced to 25 years for manslaughter. She had a roof over her head, three meals a day, and the kind of freedom from life that only prison can afford. Meanwhile, the kids bounced in and out of foster care, as the children did time in Family Services incarceration. Vicki's release date would be years after the kids were legal adults, which to Vicki meant her children would be in a position to help her out for a change. But the children, through the system, were not encouraged to perpetuate their relationship with their mother. In the end, the children were unmoored, and the library never got their dues, but Vicki adjusted well to prison life. It was a place full of women just like her, and she didn't have to give up her drug habit. The saving grace in prison was the pen pal program. Sure, there were pen pals that got off on writing incarcerated women, but there were also kind souls just offering a connection to the outside world. Sometimes, Vicki got upwards of 50 letters a month, but Claudia's correspondence was what she savored.

"Did you know?" Claudia had written in their 30th letter.

"Yes, but it was not real at the moment. I thought he was a vampire. I thought the knife was a wooden stake," Vicki wrote back. She didn't trust the prison system. She didn't trust anyone to not leak out the truth. She had given her story in the hospital, and she had stuck with it. Vicki told Claudia it was all like a nightmare, that she remembered defending herself from the vampire, and the rest was a blank until she was cuffed to a gurney in a hospital.

"What about the kids?" Claudia had written in the following letter.

Sometimes Vicki got frustrated with Claudia. Most of the time, Claudia was there for her and kept Vicki abreast of the outside world. But every once in a while, usually near the anniversary, Claudia struck out down the old haunt of, "What happened that night?"

"Jesus, does she think the story is going to change? Does she think I'm stupid?" Vicki bemoaned to the sleeping back of her roomie. Vickie pulled pen and paper out from under her mattress and began a rebuttal.

"I told you what happened. What is it you really want to know?" Vicki dashed off and put it to prison post in the morning. The next month there were no letters from Claudia. Vicki got nervous. She needed this reliable lifeline to stay sane in this place. In frustration, Vicki threw all the letters she did receive in the trash. It meant she had to check out more books from the library to give herself something to read. Vicki was more of a TV girl than a reader, but she did stumble across one book she liked, "Valley of the Dolls" by Jacqueline Susann. Vicki's roomie told her it was also a movie. Vicki finally had something to hope for, and she couldn't wait to get out of prison in 15 more years to see the film. Another month had gone by without a word from Claudia. Vicki could not take it; she decided to take the next step and write to Claudia.

"Seriously, what do you want to know? I'm lonely in here. You are the only friend I have that I don't have to worry about stabbing me in the back, like all the bitches in here. Yes, I did stab him. Yes, I did think he was a vampire. Yes, I am glad he's dead."

This short confessional letter did the trick. The next week Vicki had a letter from Claudia.

"How should I do it?" Claudia asked.

It was stark, just that one sentence in a sea of white. It was like a warped "yes" in the middle of a white canvas that won over John to Yoko in an art exhibit that would change the course of their lives. Wait, was it canvas? Vicki had heard he climbed a ladder just to read that one little word of affirmation. Is this what Claudia was looking for? Did she want moral support, or did she really want advice on killing and not getting caught? Perhaps their entire friendship was a manual in What Not to Do. For sure, Vicki had a lot to keep her mind occupied, which was always a challenge in prison. Vicki responded in what became a flurry of short notes plotting the perfect murder. At first, Vicki suggested they switch to postcards instead of letters to save paper. But Claudia pointed out that would be stupid. Yet, both ladies were foolhardy enough to commit their plans to prison mail.

"Who do you want gone?" Vicki asked.

"My father. I live with him to take care of him. I've lived here all my life. My Alvin and the Chipmunks poster is still on the wall. I'm not allowed to change anything. I still wear pigtails, which I take out when I go grocery shopping, and then I have to put them back in," Claudia wrote.

"Can't you just leave?" Vicki jotted down.

"He has a $250,000 life insurance policy," Claudia stated.

"Oh, oh. Does your Dad take any meds you could overdose him on?" Vicki asked in more of a conversational tone than not.

"He's a diabetic," Claudia replied.

The subsequent letters came and went quickly as they plotted out what would look like an accidental overdose of insulin. There was one problem. The old goat lived, and he fingered Claudia's prison pen pal as the mastermind.

Poor Claudia was sent to prison, but she did escape her childhood bedroom and leave boxes of saggy stuffed animals behind. Claudia's pale and bloated face stuck out from the tattooed faces in jail. Shortly after her arrival, Claudia got a jailhouse tat of "Vicki" on the side of her face as a medal of honor and an attempt to blend in. She continued to write to Vicki. Once Vicki got over the tough pill to swallow as an accomplice to murder while she was already serving the remaining 7 years of her original 25-year sentence, she resumed the correspondence with Claudia. She wondered how the sheltered woman was getting on in prison. Vicki decided to mail Claudia a care package, including a new toothbrush and a book. Vicki checked out "Valley of the Dolls" again from the prison library and sent it to Claudia. There would be a penalty for a "lost" book, but Vicki learned a long time ago that friends were hard to come by, and library fines were not worth fretting over.

Inside These Walls

LOUISA WAS AN EXPERT AT HIDE AND SEEK. SHE squirmed between the mattress and box springs in the spare bedroom with her Nonna's help.

"Can you breathe, Louisa?" Nonna asked.

"Yes, ssshhhh," Louisa always replied.

Until one day, her cousin Luca saw her creeping out. Busted, she sought a new super-secret hiding spot. On an ordinary Tuesday, as her siblings and cousins finished a lunch of Fontinella, salami, Italian bread, and olives at Nonna's table, Louisa searched for a new hiding spot. The others moved outside and were playing on the swing set. She watched from a window. Luca was riding his big wheel, but he stopped to pick up a worm wasting in the Sun, and he returned it to the tomato garden. From here, Louisa descended into the basement. Nonna's basement was not scary like the one at home. Grandpa had finished his basement. It had a bar, a full second kitchen, a laundry room, a bathroom, and a utility room. Everything was done in olive green and orange. The materials and the furniture had fallen off a truck from one of Grandpa's friends. The guy owed Grandpa a favor.

Louisa left the lights out. Enough sunlight made it through the glass block windows. She browsed the bottles of brown liquor on the mirrored wall and poured herself a little bit in a shot glass. She tossed it back like she watched the men in the family do on Christmas Eve. Then she coughed for a good ten minutes intermittently. She turned on the tiny bar sink and filled a see-through bottom tankard with cool water. Louisa drank it down, watching the room as it waved in the wakes of her swallows. Then, she went to the white-tiled bathroom with tiny gold flecks to pee. She traced her father's initials laid out in gold in the shower wall before she headed out for the more shadowy corners.

The back wall was made up of according-style closet doors. The closets were full of old lamps, holiday decor, and clothes that the family had outgrown from the sixties. She was ready to give up the basements' cool temperatures and seek out the stuffy attic when she noticed an unfinished piece of plywood at the back of the closet. It was not dissimilar to the roof of her dollhouse that Grandpa built. Louisa gave it a thunk and a tug. It drug backward and snagged the carpet. She stopped to inspect if the rug had been damaged. It was not too bad. It was a sturdy commercial-grade carpet.

Louisa lifted the unwieldy but lightweight wooden panel. She pushed it to the right and revealed a concrete, secret room. Louisa gave a cursory glance for spiders and bugs then stepped inside. She drug the panel door closed and sat comfortably on a concrete block. The room was clean and bare, except for a couple of cases of women's polyester dresses in blue, red, and green. It was almost patriotic. She didn't understand why Nonna would need 3 boxes of the same dress, but she didn't give it much thought; she reached the limit of her curiosity. Louisa was satisfied. This discovery was perfect. She would be able to keep her reign as hide and seek champion while Luca, her other cousins, and her little sister Sofia, all of whom would trade off trying out her old mattress haunt, failed to find her.

When Louisa was 15, she spent her summer with Nonna after Grandpa's death. She helped Nonna with the cleaning and the mourning. She learned to make stuffed artichokes and homemade sauce from the garden's tomatoes. Louisa and Nonna spent a lot of time pouring over the old photo albums, reminiscing, and bonding. Nonna went to bed by 7 p.m., which left Louisa enough time to skip a block over to Jake Hoffstedter's house. Jake spent most nights in his childhood tree house. He fished an extension cord out his bedroom window to the tree house, and he and Louisa curled up in sleeping bags, eating popcorn and watching reruns of the Twilight Zone.

Curiosity led to the inevitable, and by late July, Louisa found herself missing a period. She never wanted to see that stupid Jake Hoffstedter again. She was embarrassed. Louisa thought about confiding in Nonna, but she could not summon the courage. And she knew Nonna would whip her hide. By summer's end, Louisa had to return to home and school. She adopted autumn fashions early to cover her bump.

Louisa ate a great deal to explain her growing mid-section, but she purged in hopes of starving the baby out. She jumped on the trampoline with her little sister Sofia. Louisa snuck down into the basement on Nonna's birthday and drank six shots of bourbon. Then she skirted her parents like she had the plague so they wouldn't smell her breath. She had put a scrap of Bounce tucked away in her left cheek to try and cover the scent.

It was the new year. Nonna had asked for Louisa's assistance in taking down the tree. Louisa did most of the work while Nonna dozed off in Grandpa's old chair. It was in the middle of a Pringles commercial that Louisa was doubled-over with the first contraction. The second contraction came quickly on the heels of the first. Louisa hurried to the bathroom in the base-ment. She raised her skirt and reached into her wet panties. Her fingers came up with blood. After that, it was like instinct; Louisa squatted in the shower stall. She stared up at her father's golden initials, and she felt his disapproving frown.

Louisa bared down, pushing the early baby out. She couldn't help but push the need was too great. So far, Louisa had spent the pregnancy worrying about how to cover it up. She had yet to plan for an actual, live baby. But she needn't worry; the baby came out like a dull thud and lump on the shower stall floor. It didn't move or make a sound. It wasn't breathing. Louisa didn't want to touch it. She scooted back and away, but she was still tethered to the dead baby. This proved to be more complicated than a real baby. She could say she found the baby in the snow. Could she claim to have found a dead baby in the snow? Suddenly, the idea of finding babies in the snow seemed stupid. Louisa hyperventilated as she dug in the cabinet under the sink, looking for something to sever the tie between her and the corpse. She didn't want to know the sex, but she couldn't help but notice. She left the shell of life on the floor and began cleaning herself and the mess. Louisa lifted the baby boy in her trembling arms and tried to put him down the toilet, but he was too big for that. She fished a dirty pillowcase out of the laundry and dropped him inside. Louisa hated boys. Then she thought of it. Her good old hiding space. The secret room. Louisa's blood-stained fingers fumbled, but she eventually slid the board back. Louisa tucked the dead baby behind the three boxes of polyester dresses. She closed up the room and retraced her steps to clean up any remaining marks of blood.

Luca didn't understand where Louisa had gone wrong. She had been a sweet kid, but by her early twenties, she was already a lush. She had always seemed to be moving deeper inside herself, and as she got older, it was as if she couldn't break free of this coiled space where she was hiding. Today she was in trouble with her third DUI, her second divorce, and a lock-up in detox. Luca was the only relative still willing to give Louisa the benefit of the doubt. He showed up to Counterpoint Institute empty-handed but with a shoulder to cry on. It had been years since Luca had seen Louisa last at Nonna's house. His mother had pressured him to go over there and check to make sure Louisa was not stealing from Nonna. She was not. Nevertheless, things rapidly went downhill for Louisa with the family from there. Now, Luca was at the mental hospital to see what could be salvaged of Louisa.

"Louisa, Louisa," Luca said to the mop of stringy blonde hair.

"I'm sorry," Louisa mumbled.

"You don't have to apologize to me," Luca said. He reached out to pat her on the knee, and she jumped.

"I'm sorry. I'm sorry. I'm sorry," Louisa said and then fell silent. Luca looked at the distended outline of Louisa's face. She had been a pretty girl. What had happened to reduce Louisa to this state? Alcoholism did not run in the family. The Assanelli's were a close-knit family. What had pushed Louisa away?

Luca went to visit Nonna the following week. Nonna and Louisa had been close. Maybe Nonna knew what had happened to Louisa. Under Luca's sincere questioning, Nonna stood up and walked to the dark wood basement door. Nonna stuck her arthritic fingers in the air and motioned Luca to follow. She led him downstairs to the secret room.

"Maybe this shouldn't be a secret anymore," Nonna said. She pushed the hanging clothes aside. "Slide this paneled wall back."

Luca looked at it and gave it a shove. It moved. It was a false wall.

"Why is there a false wall here?"

"Things kept falling off Grandpa's truck," she said matter-of-factly. "Where did you think I got that endless supply of Hot Wheels when you were a kid?"

Luca was confused. Were hot Hot Wheels the source of Louisa's pain? He pushed the boxes around and found every wedding gown his mother ever wore. Nonna asked him to scoot the boxes back, and she retrieved a tightly wound bundle. She held it to her breast.

"Louisa didn't know how to swaddle it. So, I had to. I think a proper burial is what we can do for your cousin."

"Louisa's not dead, Nonna."

"No, Luca. Her son is," and she unrolled the shriveled-up corpse for Luca to see.

Luca stumbled back out of the closet with the false wall. He wanted to fall out of the family with the lies. The tiny corpse's presence in Nonna's arms pushed Luca back through time. He was face to face with the past with the decayed remains of the barely-there traces of a human being.

"Luca, she needs us. She needs us to put this to rest, so she can begin again," Nonna said.

Luca felt his jaw hanging open, he shut it up, and he called the detox hospital and asked to speak to Louisa. The head nurse gave him shit about protocol and procedure. Luca was frustrated with the family lies and the insensitive health professionals.

"She's not sub-human. She's just hurting. Let me speak with her," Luca said to the Head Nurse.

Luca gathered an old shoebox and discarded a yellowed pair of wedding shoes that had been stored there. He placed what once had been a baby into the box and handed it to Nonna to cradle. Luca dug the small grave where the swing set used to stand, next to the meager grapevine growing on the fence. Nonna rocked the 20-year-old rotten baby. The hospital had got Louisa on the line. Luca explained what was happening. Louisa sucked her breath; then gave her consent.

It was 2p.m. on a Sunday when Angelo Ford Assanelli was put to rest. Luca had checked his watch. He promised he would visit Louisa soon. Luca and Nonna retired to the kitchen for a strong cup of coffee. Nonna made small motions in the kitchen. She tipped her head over the sink to wash out a mug, and her wig slipped, landing in the drain. She reached to turn on the light overhead, but she flipped the garbage disposal on instead. Luca stopped Nonna from reaching into the grinding hole. He helped her reattach her wig, and he picked out a little bit of celery from it. Suddenly, the house felt stale and thick with nicotine and dirt that would never wash away. He looked about the kitchen, the thick grime in the corners, the deep cleaning needed, and set his Nonna in a chair. Luca opened a window. The family needed airing.

Suicide Culture

SCHADENFREUDE AND DRIPPING WITH SEX, we'd found each other in the open chasm, empty of fear, of the internet. Undone by online anonymity, we were tempted by the facade of security in a face-to-face meeting. And so, we stepped out of the shadows of our avatars and met in the open air of a crowded cafe.

We peaked quickly, and the decline was a plummet. In our last meeting, we were in costume. I was an inappropriate Alice in Wonderland, and you were a priest. The first strike, it wasn't Halloween. Next strike, we entered a local tavern we'd never been in before. A tavern filled with old-time bikers and their thick-waisted bitches. We huddled up to the bar where the inquisition began. Under our breath, we debated how many each of us could take. It turned out we couldn't take any. The problem was all we had was Hollywood bravado. I was a secretary. You were the manager at Office Depot. The fantasy of the costumes upped the tension making the moment intoxicating even without the whiskey. Unfortunately, the fall from fantasy left us beaten fools. I was molested and had a split lip. I think prejudice toward my gender saved my ass. You were beaten within an inch of your life, despite the priest get-up or maybe because of it. Thankfully, someone had called the cops.

My mother sent me an arrangement of delphiniums for the anniversary of our break-up as a wish for a sane life. Mental Illness was the umbrella my mother stood under to keep her image of me as inculpable. I pressed the flowers between the pages of our scrapbook. I've snagged the pictures and dirty text messages from my phone to build this touchstone. It was my effort to be wholesome while not forgetting. Yes, we had been into pedophilia cosplay, and we subjected each other to little tortures that would never reveal us when clothes were on. Filled with saudade, I hungered to return to our dark side. At the wrong end of a telescope, I saw myself digging an early grave. But it meant nothing if I could not share it with you. I shoveled memories out of the debris of cupidity. I forged a speculative future. Are you there? My mind blurred a delectation of hard images and our voices layered in caresses. Then the phone rang; why did I even have a landline? I refused to answer. My choleric mood applied pressure to the gawping mar in my heart. My condo was not large enough to hold these skirmishes of the past and present. I ventured out in the twilight. I walked and walked to lengthen my dreams. I curbed my strides to return home. My desire to cut our paper dolls out of the fabric of time was wanting. I did not know-how. I channeled my passion into deep-threaded signposts that were a cry for help on my arms.

And now, I am pacing in some shrink's office. I cannot stick in the chair. The shrink jokes that I'm going to wear a hole in his carpet. I'd like to fuck him on this industrial carpet. We'll see who is the boss then. I feel like a teenager: hostile and horny. I am coming of age, again. Pills and blades are not the destination; they are just methods of transportation. My fetish is not cosplay, it is not you, but it is a suicide culture where I am a statistic before I even arrive. Grounded in a circle of jerks that haven't had the will to pull the trigger, just to give voice to their desperation, to ask for help. This is the second time I've sat through group therapy. What have I learned? There are many ways to wear suicide, and everyone here stinks of failure.

Drowning

THE OUTSIDE WORLD IS BLARING. INSIDE there is a cacophony of voices. Sometimes these voices are contained in my head, and sometimes they are projected. I wander from room to room, trying to catch just what they are saying. It sounds like a distant airing of national public radio.

I've gone in hospital where someone else can care for me as I can hardly be concerned with myself. Questions tumble about inside me. Why? What's the point? Do these meds even work? It's a long, slow-suffering death this illness. Yes, it is often terminal. It is quite like drowning. Most people think suicide and drowning will mean a big display of thrashing. But like drowning, suicide is usually quiet, unseen, and painful.

Inside the hospital, the days built slowly to nothing and receded with the night watch. With the Sun comes a refresh of sedation, and coloring pages are the leaves of the day. It was a boon to go to the cafeteria for bland food and plastic spoons. It was impossible to cut the meat. If you were on suicide watch, you had to stay behind and wait for a tray grown cold, like this was in any way helping the situation. I remember no names. It doesn't matter. I was one of a penal colony submerged in waves of drugs.

I went inside voluntarily as I was suicidal with plans, and I needed help. I don't like to write that truth. I am ashamed and humiliated.

I was body checked with two females present. I felt violated, like a criminal. Their body identification fed my desecration. They were amazed at my lack of scars and tattoos. I was detached and compliant; my dignity slipped off like an old skin. I hadn't brought anything with me. So, they gave me paper towel scrubs to wear while I waited. I left my purse with my husband. He brought back a bag filled with off-limits items: clothes with drawstrings, stuffed animal, plush slippers, belts, pillow, blanket, and personal hygiene products like toothpaste, shampoo, and conditioner. Other things were kept under their lock and key: the clothes I came in, jewelry I forgot to give to my husband, and acne face wash. We could not have more things, like the battery for the remote control to the TV in the community room, which given the season of Halloween, resulted in slasher films all day. The week before, someone had swallowed the remote control battery in a suicide attempt. When it was smoke break time, smokers could have lighters, but my stuffed animal was off-limits? No one had abused the lighters; while, stuffed animals were well beyond my imagination as to their lethal capabilities, other than suffocation, which could just as easily be accomplished by one of the flat pillows.

This was getting well? Under the blare of the TV horror screams, the camera shots of splattered blood, we would play pick-up games of hangman's noose. Occasionally, there was group therapy; it involved a middle-aged woman reading a worksheet to disinterested patients. Too bad I'm not deaf. Art therapy was worse. It included paper plates with dry, crackling brown leaves and Elmer's glue-like we were five years old. I'm mentally ill, not stupid. This was my autumn. Meth addicts were familiar and alcoholics, too. Sobriety was not my issue, so often, the group therapy did not apply to me. I have bipolar disorder. Did anyone want to talk about that? Any advice on that? I understand that the DSM-5 identifies drug addiction as a mental illness. To start, drug addicts willingly took drugs. I did not take Bi-polar. It happened to me; my body betrayed itself. This seemed like a vast, insulting difference.

In for depression and suicidal thoughts, other inmates were more helpful than the majority of the staff. The orderlies were friendly and never condescending; I'll give them that. The doctors could hardly be reached. I guess they were so busy with their other doctor's duties that they didn't have time to talk to patients. From my perspective, this was not helping, just holding, like a prisoner in transfer. I wanted to go home. I wasn't healing. I was sedated.

My medication was a juggling act. Mental help was a myth. They don't know. They guess. The good ones treat patients as humans. The rest of the staff, just earning paychecks, watched us sink and then threw more drugs at us. These pills were a jettison of empty promises. I opened my mouth and inhaled deep waters.

LEAH HOLBROOK SACKETT's published books include *Swimming Middle River*, *White Knight Escort Service*, and *Raising St. Elisabeth*. Additionally, she has a short story collection, *Catawampus in Sweetgum County*, scheduled for publication in spring 2022. Leah's awards and accolades include:

- Pushcart Prize Nominee for *The Family Blend* featured in Crack the Spine
- Awarded Gold Writer Award for *Spooning* featured in Art Ascent
- Won *Two Sisters Publishing* Contest for Best Short Story: *Sticker Shock*
- Recipient of Institute for Women and Gender Studies: Creative Writing Award for *Somebody Else in Kentucky*
- Best of the Net 2020 nominee
- Short list in the Strands International Flash Fiction Competition for *The Well-Heeled Woman*

Over 75 of Leah's stories have appeared in literary journals. She is an adjunct lecturer in the English department at the University of Missouri – St. Louis, where she earned her M.F.A. Leah's stories explore journeys toward autonomy and the boundaries placed on the individual by society, family, and self.

Learn about her published fiction and non-fiction at
leaholbrooksackett.com